Aesop, Samuel Croxall

The Fables of Aesop - With a Life of the Author

Vol. 1

Aesop, Samuel Croxall

The Fables of Aesop - With a Life of the Author
Vol. 1

ISBN/EAN: 9783744767729

Printed in Europe, USA, Canada, Australia, Japan

Cover: Foto ©Andreas Hilbeck / pixelio.de

More available books at **www.hansebooks.com**

a 2

THE LIFE

OF

Æ S O P.

THE knowledge of the Egyptians was concealed in hieroglyphics and other mysterious
characters; that of the Grecians in symbols
and emblematical allusions: but Æsop, having
penetrated through the veil they had thrown
over her, brought all their mysteries to light,
and wrapped them up in fables. His life, as
recorded by Planudes and other writers of antiquity, is here faithfully presented to the
public.

He was born at Ammonius, in Phrygia the Greater; a town in itself obscure, though, from its being the birth place of Æsop, might successfully have entered into competition as a rival with those cities that with a noble emulation contended for the birth of Homer.

All agree that his person was uncommonly deformed, insomuch that the Thersites of Homer seems to be but an imperfect transcript of him. His head was long, nose flat, lips thick and pendent, a hump back, and complexion dark, from which he contracted his name (Æsopus being the same with Æthiops), large belly, and bow legs: but his greatest infirmity was, that his speech was slow, inarticulate, and very obscure. Such was the person of Æsop. But, as Nature often sets the most refulgent gems where they would be least expected, so she endowed this extraordinary man with an accomplished mind, capable of the most sublime and elevated ideas. His station in life also, as well as his person, was mean and contemptible; the former part of which was spent in the most abject poverty, and the latter in slavery, till a few years before his death.

His first master (under whose dominion he then groaned), finding him incapable of any domestic business, employed him in the field, where, not long after, he gave the first testimony of his ingenuity. It happened one day, when his master was walking in the field, that a labourer presented him with some delicious figs; which he immediately gave to the care of Agathopodus (another of his servants) till he returned from the bath. But he, in league with his fellow servant, agreed to eat them, and lay the guilt upon Æsop.—When the master returned, they loudly accused Æsop of eating the figs. The master, enraged, sent for

Æsop, and asked him what could induce him to eat the figs he had ordered to be reserved? Not answering readily in his defence, he was ordered to be punished. But, falling at his master's feet, he implored him to suspend the punishment. In which interval he ran and fetched some warm water, and drank it; then, putting his finger down his throat, he caused the water to return, for he had eaten nothing that day. He then requested that his accusers might be ordered to do the same; which, his master approving, they were told to do; and the consequence was that Æsop's innocence was apparent, and his enemies were given to the punishment they justly deserved.

The day following his master returned to the city, and Æsop was remanded to his labour; when he met two priests of Diana who had lost their way. They commanded him, in the name of Jove, to direct them into the

most regular track; which he not only performed, but refreshed them with meat; for
which kindness he gained their good wishes, as
well as their prayers.

Æsop, returning to his task, oppressed with
care and labour, lay down to sleep; and in a
dream beheld Fortune standing by him, gratifying him with volubility of language, and
the ability of wrapping up his ideas in the
form of apologues. Immediately starting up,
he exclaimed, "O wonderful! in what a charming trance have I been; for, behold, I speak
fluently, and can register each creature by its
name. This certainly is the reward of my
compliance and kindness to the strangers."
Overjoyed, he went to his labour. Having
committed some fault, Zenas (overseer of the
field) struck him.—"You are always," said
Æsop, " punishing him that offends you not.

If my master knew it, he would, no doubt, revenge these stripes." Zenas, filled with enmity, and astonished to hear him speak fluently, resolved (by way of prevention, lest he should be discharged as an unjust steward) to accuse him to his master; whom, not long after, he accosted, desiring the gods to protect him. Upon which his master inquired, what it was that discomposed him? Zenas replied, " Something wonderful in the field." The master asked, what the wonder could be? He answered, " Æsop, who was thought dumb, has now found utterance and elocution." His master observed, " This will be ruinous to thee, in whose estimation he was reputed a monster." Zenas rejoined, " What he hath spitefully spoken against me I should have buried in silence; but against you and the gods he hath uttered intolerable curses." This so incensed his master, that he ordered him to be sold for a slave, as a recompense for his ingratitude and impiety.

No sooner had Zenas got Æsop in his power than he informed him how he was to be disposed of.—To whom he replied, " Do your pleasure." Shortly after which a merchant, coming to buy cattle, met Zenas; who told him, that though he had no cattle, he had a man slave to sell. The merchant, hearing this, desired to see him. Æsop being introduced, he burst into laughter, saying, " Had I not been convinced by his voice, I should have taken him for a blown bladder. Why did you draw me aside to shock my eyes with such a deformed monster?" As he departed, Æsop desired him to stop. The merchant replied, " Be gone, you filthy cur." Æsop then requested to know for what cause he came thither. He replied, " To buy something of value, not such a worthless thing as thou art." Æsop then pressed him to buy him, promising he should find him worth his money. The merchant desired him to explain himself. " Have you at home," said Æsop, " any testy children?—I shall supply the place of bugbear, to terrify them into silence." Zenas was then asked, what he would take for that uncouth creature? " Three half-pence," said he. The merchant paid the price, observing that with nothing he had bought nothing.

When they were come near home, two of the merchant's children, seeing Æsop, testified their fear of him by crying.—" Now, sir," said Æsop, " you see the effect of my promise." As they went into the house the merchant, smiling, commanded Æsop to salute his fellow servants; who, when they beheld his deformity, ex- claimed, " What could induce my master to bring such a wretch into his family!"

Shortly after this the merchant ordered all things to be got ready for an intended journey into Asia. When they were assigning to each servant his proportion of burden, Æsop desired (it being his first time) that he might have the lightest. His request being granted, he took up the basket of bread; at which the other slaves laughed, considering that burden enough for two. But, when dinner time approached, Æsop (who had with great difficulty sustained his load) was commanded to set it down, and distribute an equal share of the bread to the other slaves.—His load being thus diminished one half, he pursued his journey with pleasure. At supper time he was again ordered to distribute of his load; after which (the basket being emptied) the next morning he led the van, and obliged those, who before had treated him with contempt, to applaud his ingenuity.

Being arrived at Ephesus, and having sold

divers of his slaves to good advantage, the merchant was persuaded to sail with the last three to Samos; namely, Cantor, a native of Cappadocia, and Grammaticus, born in Lydia; two persons of large dimensions; and Æsop, whose character was before described. Now, in order that he might the better sell the two former, he dressed them in new clothes; but (supposing no art could improve him) he clothed Æsop in sackloth, which exposed him as well to derision as to sale. Among those who came to buy was Xanthus, an eminent philosopher of Samos, attended with his scholars; who, having viewed the slaves, and seeing Æsop placed in the midst, supposed he was set there that the other two might appear to a greater advantage.

The philosopher first addressed himself to Cantor, demanding what he could perform. " All things," said he.—Xanthus then demanded what price was set upon him. The merchant replied, " a thousand half-pence." Xanthus, displeased at the price, went to the other, and asked him what he could do.—He also replied, " All things." The philosopher then asked the price of Grammaticus. He was told, " three thousand half-pence." Xanthus, thinking this also too much, declared he would buy no servants that were rated at so high a price. Upon which the scholars suggested to Xanthus to buy Æsop, saying they would pay for him.— " 'Tis not fit," said Xanthus, " that I should buy him, and you make good the payment. Besides, my wife would be much displeased to have such a mis-shapen person to wait upon her." The scholars replied, " We are not always obliged to comply with the desires of a woman; therefore let us examine this deformed creature." Xanthus, turning to Æsop, bid him be comforted. " Was I ever sad?" replied

Æsop. "Of what place are you a native?" said the philosopher. "I am a negro," said Æsop. "I do not ask you that, but where you were born?" Æsop answered, "Of my mother."—"Neither did I ask that," said Xanthus. "But what place were you born in?"—"My mother never informed me whether above or below."—"What can you perform?"—"Nothing," replied Æsop; "the two former having told you they can do all things, there remains nothing for me to do."—"Are you willing," said Xanthus, "that I should buy you?"—"You ought," answered Æsop, "to judge for yourself. Why do you ask me? If you are willing, pay down the price, and make an end of the business."—"If I buy you," said Xanthus, "you will try to escape."—"If I do," said Æsop, "I shall not come to you for advice, as you do now to me."—"But thou art deformed!"—"A philosopher," replied Æsop,

" should not only view the body, but examine the mind." The scholars, pleased with his ingenious replies, again requested Xanthus to buy him. He therefore asked the merchant what price was set upon him; who answered, " Surely thy design is to debase my commodities. Thou hast declined the best to take the worst." However, Xanthus, desirous of buying him, again asked the price; which, when known, the scholars paid, and Xanthus took him into possession.

When they came near home Xanthus commanded Æsop to wait in the porch, lest his deformity should offend his wife; whom Xanthus thus addressed—" Mistress, you shall have no cause for the future to be discontented, for there is a servant in the porch as handsome as ever was beheld." At this the maids smiled, and contended who should first oblige him. The wife of Xanthus ordered

one of them to fetch him. Æsop, overhear-
ing her, prepared to enter. The maid, amazed
at his deformity, cried, " Art thou he?"—" Yes,
sure," said Æsop. " Enter not," replied the
maid, " unless you mean to frighten us all
out of the house." But Æsop persisted, and
appeared before his mistress; who, upon seeing him, thus addressed Xanthus:—" What
monster is this you have brought?—Discharge
him instantly." At the same time declaring
he had much offended her, and desiring he
would return that with which she had en-
riched him, and she would abandon that unhappy mansion. On this Xanthus rebuked
Æsop, who had discovered so much ingenuity
before, that he was so silent now.—" Cast
her off," said Æsop. " Away with you, villain," replied he. " My love and my life is so
incorporated into hers, as if one heart alone
managed two bodies." At which Æsop, stamp-

ing, said that Xanthus was under the dominion of his wife; and turning to his mistress, said, " You, madam, would have had the philosopher have brought you a young, handsome fellow, whose attractions might feed your vanity, but at the same time might endanger his reputation:—Oh, Euripides, thy mouth was a golden one, for these words came out of it!—' Great is the effort of the sea when its waves swell into sedition, and obey no law; and the flame or impression of devouring fire, poverty, is a ruinous condition; and there are many things intolerable, but nothing equal to an impetuous woman.' You, being the wife of a philosopher, should not be attended by such persons as would bring philosophy itself into disrepute."—She, being unable to contradict him, asked Xanthus, where he had purchased this beauty. " The handsomeness of his ingenuity," said she, " doth recompense for the deformity of his person: my dislike of him is extinguished."—"Your mistress," said Xanthus to Æsop, "is now reconciled." Æsop ironically replied, "'Tis a difficult matter sure to appease a woman."—"For the future," said Xanthus, "be silent; I bought you to obey, not to contradict."

The day following, Xanthus, going to the garden to buy herbs, commanded Æsop to accompany him. When the gardener had gathered the herbs, he intrusted them to Æsop. When they were paid for, the gardener asked Xanthus, what was the natural reason that the herbs which he planted did not improve with that quick and active growth, as those which were Nature's voluntary production? Xanthus not being able to answer the question, thus replied, "It thus happened from that order and series of Providence that threaded together inferior causes and their effects."—At

which Æsop smiled.—" Do you laugh at me?"
said Xanthus.—" I laugh at you," answered
he, " and not you only, but him that taught
you."—Upon which Xanthus, addressing himself to the gardener, said, " It is not fit for me,
who have disputed in learned auditories, to unravel questions in a garden.—My servant here
will solve the difficulty." The gardener replied,
" Is there any knowledge treasured up in this
sordid vessel?"—At which Æsop was offended,
and asked the gardener this question. " When
a widow is engaged in second nuptials she is
mother to the issue of her first marriage, but
stepmother to the children of her second husband. Those, to whom by the proper obligations of Nature her affections are intitled, she
affects and values more than those to whom
she is mother only by accidental relation.—So
it is here—the earth is a stepmother to those
plants which are incorporated into her womb

by art, but a mother to those which are her own free production." The gardener was so well satisfied with his reply, that he gave him liberty to gather what herbs he might at any time want, as a recompense.

Some days after this, Xanthus, having met with some friends at the bath, and intending to invite them to dinner, ordered Æsop to go directly home, and boil some lentils. He went, as enjoined, and only boiled one. Xanthus, after bathing, accordingly invited his friends, informing them, that though their fare would be but scanty, yet he was confident they would take the will for the deed.—When they came home Xanthus ordered Æsop to bring something to drink; who, taking some water from the stream of the bath, presented it to Xanthus.—At which he was offended, and asked Æsop where he brought it from? " From the bath," said Æsop. Xanthus, on account of his friends, concealed his anger, and called for a bason, which Æsop having brought, stood still.—Xanthus asked him, " Do you not wash?" He replied, " 'Tis for you to command, me to obey." But to put water in the bason was no part of the command. Upon which Xanthus asked his friends whether they thought he had bought a servant?—Who replied that, in their opinion, he had rather purchased a master.—Xanthus now asked if dinner was ready? When Æsop, putting the lentil into a shell, presented it to his master; who, having tried if it was boiled enough, ordered him to serve up the rest. Æsop immediately put the broth into saucers, and brought them to Xanthus; who asked where the lentils were? " You have it already," replied Æsop. " Did you boil but one?" said his master. " No more, sir," said Æsop; " your command was in the singular

number." At which Xanthus, incensed, exclaimed, "This fellow is enough to drive me
mad! but, that I may not deceive my friends,
go instantly, and buy four hogs' feet, and boil
them." Which Æsop cheerfully did. Now,
while they were boiling, Xanthus, wishing to
find some cause of complaint in Æsop's absence, took out one of the feet; which Æsop
on his return missed, and, suspecting the design, ran to an adjacent hog-sty; and, cutting
off one of the feet of a fatted hog, singed it,
and put it into the pot. Xanthus, suspecting
that Æsop, on the discovery, would run away,
put the foot in again. So that, when Æsop
came to serve them up on the table, he found
there were five. Upon which Xanthus inquired by what means they were multiplied.
Æsop answered by asking, "How many feet
have two hogs?"—His master replied, "Eight."
—"Here, then," said Æsop, "are five present,

and yon fatted hog hath the other three."—
Xanthus, being more enraged at this, exclaimed, " Did not I say this fellow would
drive me mad!"

Shortly afterwards one of the scholars invited Xanthus and his fellow students to a
feast. Where Xanthus, wishing to reconcile
the difference he had occasioned when he first
returned, sent Æsop with a choice dish to his
mistress, telling him to give it to her that
loved him best. Æsop went; and, seating himself in the porch, called his mistress, and shewed her the present Xanthus had sent to her
that loved him best. " But this," said he,
" madam, is not for you."—Then, calling his
master's bitch Lycæna, he cast it down, and
bid her eat it. At his return Xanthus asked
him whether he had done as he was ordered?
He said, " Yes, and she swallowed it in my presence." His master then inquired what she

said. "Nothing to me," said Æsop, "but to you she returns her thanks." This so offended his mistress, that she determined to leave the house. In the mean time, while they were all heated with wine, one of the company asked, when would be the time of the greatest confusion among mortals? Æsop replied, "When the dead rise, and attempt to trace out their ancient possessions." At which the scholars smiled. Another asked why sheep die so calmly, and swine with such an offensive noise?—"The sheep," answered Æsop, "being used to be shorn, are silent, and expect nothing but what is customary; but swine, unaccustomed to be handled, when they are killed, make an hideous noise." The scholars were so pleased with his answers that they burst into laughter. Supper being over, Xanthus returned home, and would have saluted his wife; but she, being highly offended at

what had passed, told him she would have nothing to say to him, who, instead of sending
her his dainties, had sent them to his dog.—
Xanthus, surprised, asked Æsop to whom he
had presented them. Who replied, "To her
that loves you best." Then, calling the spaniel,
"This is she," said he, "for, though you load
her with stripes, yet still she fawns upon and
accompanies you.—You should have told me
to present them to your wife."—"You are
now convinced, mistress," said Xanthus, "it
was not my fault that the present miscarried.
Bear the disappointment with patience, and I
will take an opportunity of avenging it upon
Æsop." But this did not satisfy his wife. She
therefore went to her father; which caused
Æsop to triumph, saying, "Now, sir, you see
which loves you best."

After this Æsop, observing his master un-
easy on account of his wife's departure, told

him not to be unhappy, for that he would soon bring her back again. For which purpose he set off to market, and purchased fowls, geese, &c. With these he intentionally went to the house where his mistress resided, and asked the servants if they had any thing to sell that would add to the magnificence of a wedding feast he was about to provide. They inquiring whose marriage was going to be celebrated, he replied, " Xanthus means to celebrate his second nuptials to-morrow." This intelligence soon reached the ear of his wife; and filled her so with jealousy that she flew home, and declared that no second espousals of his should be established but upon her urn. Thus Æsop, who was the occasion of her departure, was the cause of her hasty return.

Not long after Xanthus invited his scholars to dinner, and ordered Æsop to furnish the feast with the choicest dainties; who, while fulfilling the command of his master, was studying how to expose his folly. He therefore laid out the money in tongues, which he served up accompanied with a poignant sauce.

The scholars much commended this first course, as it furnished them with matter for conversation: but the second and third being the same, the guests were astonished as well as their master; who inquired if there was nothing provided but tongues? Æsop replied, " Nothing else."—" Thou lump of deformity," said Xanthus, " did not I command you to prepare the choicest dainties?"—" Sir," said Æsop, " your reproof before philosophers deserves my thanks.—What excels the tongue? It is the great channel of learning and philosophy. By this noble organ addresses, commerce, contracts, eulogies, and marriages, are completely established. On this moves life itself. Therefore nothing is equal to the tongue." The scholars, departing, declared that the philosophy of Æsop excelled that of Xanthus.

Some time after this Xanthus, perceiving the dissatisfaction of his scholars, told them it was not his design so to have treated them. " But now," said he, " I have ordered my servant to procure the worst meats for supper." Æsop, however, (constant to his purpose) again provided tongues. Xanthus, more incensed still, asked him if this was the entertainment he had ordered? To which Æsop replied, that he had exactly fulfilled his commands. " For what," said he, " is worse than the tongue?—Is it not frequently the ruin of empires, cities, and private connections?—Is it not the conveyance of calumnies and forgeries?—In short, is it not the grand disturber of civil society?" When the scholars heard his reply, they declared that the deformity of his body was but the transcript of his distorted and irregular manners; and gave Xanthus a caution, lest his behaviour should drive him out of his mind. To whom Æsop observed, that their speech betrayed their malice, by endeavouring to cause discontent between him and his master.

Xanthus, still desirous to revenge himself for these affronts, again sought for cause to complain of Æsop; and commanded him (since he had accused the scholars of officiousness) to find a man that regarded nothing. The next day, while traversing the streets, Æsop discovered one sitting in a negligent posture, void of reflection. This man Æsop accosted, and invited to dinner with his master. The clown, without hesitation, followed him, and sat down at his master's table in his mean attire. Xanthus immediately asked who this guest was? Æsop replied, " It is a person regardless."

Xanthus then desired his wife to wash the
stranger's feet, thinking he would not permit
her.—But, when she offered, the clown care-
lessly stretched out his feet for the purpose,
and suffered her to perform the office. Xanthus
next ordered him a goblet of wine, which he
readily drank off. When the meat was set before him, Xanthus complained that it was not
enough seasoned; but the clown said, he
thought it was very agreeable. Whereupon
Xanthus, troubled because he could not dis-
compose him, ordered the cheesecakes to be
brought, which the stranger also disposed of.
Upon this, Xanthus blamed the baker for not
mingling honey and pepper in the cheesecakes. The baker said it was not his fault,
but that of his mistress. Xanthus then said,
if it was so, that she should be instantly burnt
alive, thinking the clown would attempt her
rescue. But he, seeing no occasion for so pro-

digious a passion, desired Xanthus to wait
until he brought his wife also, that they might
both suffer together. Upon this Xanthus acknowledged that Æsop had punctually fulfilled
his command, for which he would shortly grant
him his freedom.

The next day Xanthus sent Æsop to the
bath, to inform him what company was there.
As he was going he met the city prætor; who
(knowing him to be the servant of Xanthus)
asked him where he was going. Æsop answered, " I do not know."—At which the prætor was offended, and ordered him to prison
for speaking so impertinently. As they were
taking him away, he cried out, " Oh, prætor, did not I tell you I did not know where
I was going?"—The prætor, pleased with the
reply, dismissed him: and Æsop went on his
errand. Observing that many stumbled, both
going in and coming out of the bath, at a

stone which lay at the entrance, and that only one attempted to lay it aside, he went home, and told his master there was but one person in the bath. Xanthus arriving, and seeing a multitude, asked him the reason of his false information. Æsop told him, there was a great stone lay at the entrance, over which many stumbled, but only one removed the obstacle; so that there was only one man, the rest being little better than cyphers.

· Not long after, on a day fixed by Xanthus and other philosophers for public rejoicing, Xanthus having drank freely, was raised into a passion, being worsted in some dispute that had arisen. Which Æsop observing, said, " Master, Bacchus is the parent of three evils.— The first is voluptuousness, the second intemperance, the third calumny or reproach; of which you, being engaged in drink, should beware."—At last, Xanthus being intoxicated, one of the scholars asked him if it was possible to drink off the sea. " Very easy," said Xanthus, " I will engage to perform it myself." Upon which they laid a wager; and having exchanged rings, departed. The day following Xanthus missed his ring, and asked Æsop what was become of it. " I know not," said he, " but this I am confident of—we must not stay here ; for yesterday, when disguised with liquor, you betted your whole fortune that you would drink off the ocean; and, to bind the wager, you exchanged your ring." Xanthus replied, " What could I engage less?—But can you contrive how to get rid of it."— " To perform it," said Æsop, " is impossible; but how to avoid it I will shew you—When you meet again, be as confident as ever, and order a table to be placed on the shore, and persons prepared to lave the ocean with cups; and, when the multitude are assembled, ask what was the wager. The reply will be, that you engaged to drink up the sea: then do you address them thus, ' Ye citizens of Samos, you are not ignorant that many rivers discharge themselves into the sea. My agreement was to drink up the ocean, and not those streams. If you, then, can obstruct their course, I am ready to perform my engagement.' Xanthus, being pleased with the expedient, when the people assembled, acted and said as Æsop had instructed him ; for which he was highly applauded. When the scholar fell at his feet, and owned himself wrong ; at the same time requesting that the wager might be dissolved : which Xanthus, at the desire of the Samians, granted.

Æsop, on his return home, intimated to Xanthus how much he had merited-his freedom, which so offended Xanthus, that he had bid him go to the door; and, if there were two crows in sight, to tell him, for it was an auspicious omen; but, if he beheld but one, it would be a bad one. Æsop returned, and told him he saw two perched on a tree. But, when Xanthus went out, one of them was gone. Upon which he called Æsop an ungrateful villain, observing that his whole aim was to make him an object of ridicule, for which he should now be scourged.—Æsop, groaning with his stripes, addressed one who entered to sup with his master in a sad accent thus, " You that beheld one crow, are rewarded with a supper; and I, that discovered two, am recompensed undeservedly." Which ingenious address so softened Xanthus, that he forbad the continuance of his punishment.

Shortly after, Xanthus designing to entertain the philosophers and orators, commanded Æsop to stand at the gate, and to admit none but wise men. At the appointed time several

came to the gate, requesting admittance : but
Æsop put this question to them all—" What
stirs the dog?" At which they were much
offended, supposing he meant to give them
that appellation. At last one came who made
this reply to his question, " His ears and his
tail." Æsop, satisfied with the answer, admitted him, and conducted him to his master,
saying there was only one philosopher had
desired admittance. The day following, when
they met at the schools, they reproached
Xanthus with treating them contemptuously,
by permitting Æsop to stand at the gate and
salute them with the opprobrious epithet of
" dogs." Xanthus asked if they were serious.
They replied, they were. Upon which Æsop
was called, and asked how he dared to affront
his friends?—To which he replied, " Did you
not tell me that none but philosophers should
be admitted?"—" And what are these?" said

Xanthus, " do they not merit that character?"
" By no means," said Æsop, " for, when they
came to the gate, I demanded of them—What
stirs the dog? And but one among them all
gave me a proper answer." Upon this all
agreed that Æsop had acted strictly as his
master commanded him.

One day, when Xanthus, accompanied by
Æsop, went to visit the monuments, and to
amuse himself with the inscriptions, Æsop,
seeing these letters on one of them, sc. " α, β,
δ, ο, ε, ϑ, χ," shewed them to Xanthus, asking
him their meaning. Who, after serious consideration, confessed he knew not. " Master,"
said Æsop, " if by these characters I trace out
a treasure, what reward shall I receive?" Xanthus answered, " thy freedom, and half the
treasure." Then Æsop, having dug the earth
four feet from the stone, found it; and, giving it to his master, claimed his reward.

" No," said Xanthus, " not till I can unravel the mystery, the knowledge of which will be more than the treasure." Æsop told him a prudent man had engraven them, and the sense was this:—" α going, β, paces, δ, four, ο digging, ε thou shalt find, Ϥ a treasure, χ of gold!" Xanthus answered, " It will be more to my interest to keep thee than to let thee go."—" Then," said Æsop, " I will prove that the gold belongs to the king of Bizantium."— " How do you prove it?" said his master. " Thus," replied he, " α restore, β to the king, δ Dionysius, ο which, ε thou hast found, Ϥ treasure, χ of gold." Upon this Xanthus request- ed Æsop to accept the half, as a reward for his silence. Æsop replied, " I receive not this as the effect of your bounty, but of his who concealed it; for this is the genuine sense of the letters—α taking, β go your way, δ divide, ο which, ε you have found, Ϥ the treasure."

Xanthus replied, " Come, depart; the moiety of the gold, and your freedom, shall be your reward." As they returned, Xanthus (fearing Æsop would discover the affair) commanded that they should take him to prison. As they were taking him away, Æsop exclaimed, " Do the solemn promises of philosophers, and their specious intimation of liberty, end in prison and fetters?" Upon which Xanthus ordered his release, observing that what he had said was true; though he was confident, when he had got his freedom, he would do all that lay in his power to injure him. Æsop answered, " In spite of all your artifices, I shall obtain my liberty."

Soon after this, on a day appointed for general festivity by the citizens of Samos, an eagle descended, snatched up the public ring, and afterward dropped it into the lap of a slave. The astonished Samians applied to

Xanthus to unfold the mystery; who, knowing himself incapable, was very much de-
jected. Æsop, perceiving this, asked what made
him so unhappy. " To-morrow, when you
appear in public," says he, " tell the Samians,
that you are not dexterous in these matters,
but you have a servant that is." To this Xanthus agreed, and accordingly the next day
Æsop was called forth.—But, when they saw
him, they smiled, asking contemptuously,
" How can such a deformed creature unfold
this great mystery?" Æsop, waving his hand,
replied, " Ye citizens of Samos, ye should not
only view the front of the house, but the
tenant also; for frequently an upright and
understanding soul dwells in a deformed and
disordered body: and you know it is not the
shape of the cask that men admire, but the
wine concealed therein."—Hearing this, they
desired him to proceed; wherefore he con-

tinued, " Ye Samians, it rests with you to judge between the master and the servant. If I do not unfold the mystery concealed in this signal accident, let stripes be my reward ; but, if the master be outvied by the discovery, then let my freedom be given me." Upon this they insisted that Xanthus should give Æsop his freedom. Xanthus making no reply, the city prætor addressed him thus :—" If you do not grant the request of the people, I will declare Æsop free." Whereupon Xanthus declared Æsop free, and the city crier proclaimed it.—Then said Æsop to his master, " In spite of all your malice, I have obtained my freedom." And then, addressing the people, he thus unfolded the mystery ;—" Ye citizens of Samos! the eagle, you know, is the monarch of birds ; and, as the public ring was dropped into the lap of a slave, it seems to forebode that some of the adjacent kings will attempt to overthrow your established laws, and entomb your liberty in slavery."

This filled the Samians with grief. Shortly after, letters arrived from Crœsus of Lydia, requiring the Samians to pay tribute, or else prepare to suffer the calamities of a destructive war.

Upon which a public council was called, and Æsop was requested to give his advice; who thus addressed them : " We have," said he, " but two objects before us.—The one is liberty; which in the beginning is rough and difficult, but in the end smooth and easy : the other is bondage; whose beginning is easy, but the conclusion fatal and calamitous." The Samians, when they heard this, declared, that, as they were at present free, so they and their liberty would stand or fall together. And with this resolute reply dismissed the ambassadors. Crœsus, being informed of their resolution, determined to go to war with them. But the ambassadors advised him first to send for Æsop, with a promise that the tribute should be suspended, and then perhaps he might reduce them; but that, as long as they were strengthened with the counsel of Æsop, he would not be able.—Crœsus took their advice, and sent for him upon those conditions. The Samians, being well satisfied, agreed to give him up. But, when Æsop heard of it, he thus addressed them,—"Ye citizens of Samos, I am ready to prostrate myself at the feet of Crœsus, but first I will tell you a tale.—The wolves commenced war with the sheep, but the sheep were secured by the generous protection of the dogs; on which the wolves sent ambassadors to the sheep, to this end, that, if they desired peace, they should give up their dogs. The timorous and unwary sheep agreed to it, and sent away their protectors.—The wolves immediately destroyed their dogs, and then the sheep fell an easy prey."——The Samians, comprehending his meaning, refused to let Æsop go, but he resolved to accompany the ambassadors.

When they arrived at Lydia, they presented Æsop. As soon as the king saw him he was angry; despising the idea that so despicable a person should by his counsels prevent him from conquering the Samians.—Æsop, observing his astonishment, said, " Mighty sir! since neither by force nor necessity, but my own free will, I give myself up, I request your attention.—A certain man, having gathered many locusts, killed them; and having with them taken a grashopper, she thus bespoke him:—' Sir, do not kill me, for I am no ways destructive, my whole employment being to charm to sleep the weary traveller.'—Upon which he let her go.—Thus I, O king, prostrate before you, desire my life may be the monument of your mercy, since it cannot be prejudicial to any man; for in this deformed body you shall find an exalted mind." Crœsus replied, " Æsop, not only thy life, but a fortune, shall be the proof of my beneficence. Demand, therefore, what you please, and it shall be granted."—" Oh king," said Æsop, " be reconciled to the Samians." The king replied, " I am." And shortly after sent Æsop back with letters of reconciliation. On his arrival the citizens, crowned with garlands, saluted him, rejoicing to find that peace was re-established.

He not long after departed from Samos; and, after passing through many kingdoms, and disputing with several philosophers, at last arrived at Babylon; where he soon gained the esteem of king Lycerus. In those days it was usual for nations to send philosophical questions to each other, subject to a fine if they could not resolve them.—Now Æsop, unfolding those sent to king Lycerus, improved the reputation of the king. He also, in the king's name, proposed many; which the neighbouring kings were not able to resolve.

Æsop, being childless, had adopted a nobleman named Eunus for his heir, and sought the favour of the king in his behalf. But one day, surprising him with his concubine, he discarded him. In revenge for which, Eunus forged letters from Æsop to the philosophers of another kingdom, and presented them to king Lycerus; in which it appeared that Æsop wished to render them services in preference to the king.

The king, believing the imposture, without examining into the truth of it, ordered Hermippus to put Æsop to death. But he, being in friendship with Æsop, concealed him

in a sepulchre. The king gave Æsop's estates
to Eunus.

Not long after this, Nectenabo, king of
Egypt, hearing Æsop was dead, sent a letter
to Lycerus, requiring artificers who could
erect a tower which should neither touch
heaven nor earth, and one that could resolve
all that was demanded; on the accomplish-
ment of which he would pay him tribute;
but, in case of failure, he would exact it of
him. After the king had read the letter he
cried out, " Æsop, the pillar of my kingdom,
is dead!" Now Hermippus, hearing the king
deplore his loss, informed him he had not
performed his command, but had preserved
the life of Æsop; well knowing that the king
himself would in the end be grieved.

At which the king rejoiced, and sent for
Æsop; who, after having established his innocence, was again received into favour, and

Eunus was condemned to die; but, on the intercession of Æsop, his life was spared. Now, as soon as the king of Egypt's letter was shewn to Æsop, he desired that this message might be returned—' that, after winter was expired, one should appear who would not only erect the tower, but answer every question demanded.' Which was immediately dispatched. Æsop, having re-adopted Eunus, admonished him to this effect—" My son, worship God, and honour the king; make thyself a terror to thine enemies, and useful to thy friends. Pray that thine enemies may be indigent, that they may not offend thee; and thy friends opulent, that they may be able to assist thee. Be constant to thy consort, lest thy inconstancy should make her so. Be slow to speak and swift to hear. Envy not those who do well. So manage thy domestic affairs that those who fear may love. Be not ashamed to learn. Trust not thy secrets to a woman, lest she should be insolent. Let to-day's stock be the pledge of to-morrow's store. Be gentle to all. Discard parasites and whisperers. Always act as thou mayest have no cause to repent."—These sayings had such an effect upon Eunus, that he shortly after died with remorse and compunction.

The winter being nearly expired, Æsop procured four young eagles; which he taught to carry baskets with little children in them, and to obey their command; and, having prepared for his journey into Egypt, in a short time set off, taking the eagles with him.

Nectenabo, being told that Æsop was arrived, expressed his surprise, having understood that he was dead. The next day all his officers were assembled, dressed in white robes; and the king in his royal attire and imperial diadem. When seated on his throne he sent for Æsop, and asked him, to what he resembled him, and those who surrounded the throne? Æsop replied, "You resemble the vernal sun, and your attendants a fruitful harvest."—With which answer the king was greatly pleased.—The day following the king appeared in white, and his retinue in purple; when Æsop was asked the same question: to which he answered, "You are an emblem of the sun, and those that stand round a type of effused beams."—Then Nectenabo inquired his opinion of his kingdom, and whether he did not think it preferable to that of Lycerus. "Do not flatter yourself," said Æsop, "though your kingdom may shine like the rays of the sun, yet, if put into competition with his, it would soon fade." Nectenabo, applauding his answer, asked where they were that could erect the tower. "They are ready," said Æsop, "if you have appointed the place."

Upon which the king shewed him a spacious plain. Then Æsop produced the eagles, with the children in the baskets; and, giving them their working instruments, commanded the eagles to fly; who, being raised in the air, demanded the necessary materials.—Nectenabo, hearing their request, said to Æsop, " I have no men that can fly."—Æsop replied, " How then can you think of engaging in a contest with king Lycerus, who is stored with such?" Nectenabo acknowledged himself subdued.

Shortly after he sent for several sages from Heliopolis, to ask Æsop a variety of questions. One of the Heliopolitans at the banquet said to Æsop, " I am employed by one of our deities to ask you this question."—" You discover your ignorance," said Æsop, " by diminishing the knowledge of one of your gods." A second put this question, desiring Æsop to explain it.—' There is a vast temple, and a column supporting twelve magnificent cities, each of which is sustained with thirty rafters, and constantly circulated by two women.'— To this Æsop answered,—'The temple is this world, the cities the months, the rafters the days of the month, and the day and night are the two women who successively attend each other.'

The day following Nectenabo summoned his friends, and confessed that the tribute exacted by Lycerus was due to the ingenuity of Æsop.—One of them replied, "We will try him again with questions that were never heard of."—"And I," said Æsop, " will answer them."

He then departed, and prepared a schedule, whereon was engrossed—" Nectenabo confesses he is indebted a thousand talents to Lycerus;" and in the morning presented it to the king; who, paying him the money, observed that

Lycerus was fortunate to have his kingdom supported by so sagacious a person.—He then dismissed him, bidding him farewell.

Æsop, having digested the whole into a narrative, returned to Babylon, and presented it with the tribute to Lycerus; who was so well pleased, that he commanded an elegant statue to be erected to his memory.

Shortly after he obtained leave of the king to sail into Greece, upon condition that he should return to Babylon.—Having surveyed the different provinces, and obtained an eminent character, he set off for Delphos, where the temple of Apollo stood.—But here they paid but little attention to his eloquence: observing which, Æsop said, " Ye citizens of Delphos, you justly resemble the wood that floats on the sea; which at a distance appears something worth, but when it approaches we are disappointed. So I, when at a great distance from your city, did admire you, but now am led to think you the most useless among men."—Hearing this, they were afraid that he would, at his departure, speak disrespectfully of them; they therefore determined to ensnare and destroy him.—For which end they took a golden cup out of the temple, and concealed it in Æsop's baggage; who, unsuspecting, departed to Phocide. The Delphians pursued him, and there charged him with sacrilege.—He denied the fact; but they untied his baggage, found the cup, and discovered it to the city.—Æsop, now seeing through their malicious stratagem, desired they would not deprive him of his life. But they first condemned him to prison, and then to death.—Æsop, unable to extricate himself, deplored his fate in the prison: while he was complaining, one Demas (a friend) asked him the cause of his violent sorrow.—Æsop replied, " A woman, having lately buried her husband, wept daily over his grave. One, who was plowing not far off, fell in love with her; and, leaving his oxen, went to the grave, and mourned with her. She asked why he wept. ' Because,' replied he, ' I have lately buried an amiable wife, and find it gives me ease.'—' Such is my fate,' said the woman. ' Then,' said he, ' as we are united in trouble, why should we not be joined in marriage, since we love each other?'—While they were thus engaged some villain took away his oxen; upon which he went home, and wept much. The woman inquired, why he wept now. He replied, ' I have just cause to weep.'—So I, after having escaped many dangers, have cause to weep that I cannot extricate myself from this." The Delphians then came, and dragged him to the verge of a craggy precipice; when Æsop thus addressed them:—

" When beasts did parley, the mouse, being
intimate with the frog, invited her to supper
in the storehouse of a rich man, desiring her
to make herself welcome.—After this the frog
invited the mouse; and, that he might not
be tired with swimming, she tied his leg to
hers. This done, they endeavoured to go
across the stream; but, before they were half
over, the mouse was drowned; and, when
dying, declared the frog was the cause, and
that some more powerful than themselves
would avenge his death.—The eagle, behold-
ing the mouse floating on the water, snatched
at him, and with him took the frog; thus both
fell a prey to the eagle.—So I, who am ready
to fall a victim to your injustice, shall not
want an avenger; for all Greece and Babylon
will unite for that purpose."

But all this was of no avail; neither his
attempt to shelter himself in the temple.

They still continued dragging him to the precipice; when he again addressed them:—" Ye citizens of Delphos, the hare, being pursued by the eagle, retreated into the nest of the hornet.—The hornet implored the eagle to have pity on the hare. The eagle repulsed the hornet, and destroyed the hare. The hornet traced out the nest of the eagle, and demolished her eggs. The next time the eagle built her nest higher; but the hornet still pursued, and again destroyed them. The third time the eagle soared, and deposited her eggs between the knees of Jupiter, invoking his protection. The hornet, · composing a ball of dirt, dropped it into Jupiter's lap; who, forgetting the eggs, shook all off together.—Being informed by the hornet that this was in revenge for a former injury, he endeavoured to reconcile them, lest the progeny of his favorite bird should be destroyed.—But, the

hornet persisting, he respited the hatching of
the eagles till the time when the hornets sally
forth.—And you, citizens of Delphos, despise
not this deity, from whom I have implored
refuge."

Now Æsop, perceiving they continued still
deaf to his entreaties, sternly, and for the last
time, bespoke them thus: " Ye cruel and ob-
durate men, a certain husbandman, growing
aged, who had never beheld the city, desired
his servants to convey him thither, that he
might see it before he died. As he went he
was overtaken by a violent storm and gloomy
darkness, so that the asses which drew the
carriage mistook the way, and guided him to
a precipice; where, being upon the verge of
approaching ruin, he thus exclaimed, ' Oh
Jove, what injury have I committed, that
hath incensed thee to cause this misfortune;
especially that I should owe my death not to

generous horses, nor active mules, but to dull and despicable asses?"—"And this," said Æsop, " is my unhappy fate, to fall, not by the hands of persons of worth and abilities, but by those of the vilest and most worthless of men."— This said, the Delphians threw him from the precipice, and he perished.

Not long after, a destructive pestilence having raged among them, they were told by the oracle, that it was the expiation of Æsop's unjust tragedy. Wherefore, in order to avert the judgment, they erected a pompous monument over his bones.

But when the principles of Greece and the sages were informed of the catastrophe, and having maturely weighed the fact, they severely revenged the innocent effusion of Æsop's blood.

ÆSOP'S FABLES.

FABLE I.

THE COCK AND THE JEWEL.

A BRISK young Cock, in company with two or three pullets, his mistresses, raking upon a dunghill for something to entertain them with, happened to scratch up a Jewel. He knew what it was well enough, for it sparkled with an exceeding bright lustre; but, not knowing what to do with it, endeavoured to cover his ignorance under a gay contempt:

so, shrugging up his wings, shaking his head, and putting on a grimace, he expressed himself to this purpose:—' Indeed, you are a very fine thing; but I know not any business you have here. I make no scruple of declaring that my taste lies quite another way; and I had rather have one grain of dear delicious barley, than all the jewels under the sun.'

APPLICATION.

There are several people in the world that pass, with some, for well-accomplished gentlemen, and very pretty fellows, though they are as great strangers to the true uses of virtue and knowledge as the Cock upon the dunghill is to the real value of the Jewel. He palliates his ignorance by pretending that his taste lies another way. But, whatever gallant airs people may give themselves upon these occasions, without dispute, the solid advantages of virtue, and the durable pleasures of learning, are as much to be preferred before other objects of the senses, as the finest brilliant diamond is above a barley-corn. The greatest blockheads would appear to understand what at the same time they affect to despise: and nobody yet was ever so vicious, as to have the impudence to declare, in public, that virtue was not a fine thing.

But still, among the idle, sauntering young fellows of the age, who have leisure as well to cultivate and improve the faculties of the mind, as to dress and embellish the body, how many are there who spend their days in raking after new scenes of debauchery, in comparison of those few who know how to relish more reasonable entertainments! Honest, undesigning good sense is so unfashionable, that he must be a bold man who, at this time of day, attempts to bring it into esteem.

How disappointed is the youth who, in the midst of his amorous pursuits, endeavouring to plunder an outside of bloom and beauty, finds a treasure of impenetrable virtue concealed within! And why may it not be said, how delighted are the fair sex when, from among a crowd of empty, frolic, conceited admirers, they find out, and distinguish with their good opinion, a man of sense, with a plain, unaffected person, which, at first sight, they did not like!

FABLE II.

THE WOLF AND THE LAMB.

ONE hot, sultry day, a Wolf and a Lamb happened to come, just at the same time, to quench their thirst in the stream of a clear silver brook, that ran tumbling down the side of a rocky mountain. The Wolf stood upon the higher ground, and the Lamb at some distance from him down the current. However, the Wolf, having a mind to pick a quarrel with him, asked him, what he meant by disturbing the water, and making it so muddy that he could not drink; and, at the same time, demanded satisfaction. The Lamb, frightened at this threatening charge, told him, in a tone as mild as possible, that, with humble submission, he could not conceive how that could be; since the water which he drank, ran down from the Wolf to him, and therefore it could not be disturbed so far up the stream. 'Be that as it will,' replies the Wolf, 'you are a rascal, and I have been told that you treated me with ill language behind my back, about half a year ago.'—Upon my word,' says the Lamb, 'the time you mention was before I was born.' The Wolf, finding it to no purpose to argue any longer against truth, fell into a great passion, snarling and foaming at the mouth, as if he had been mad; and drawing nearer to the Lamb, 'Sirrah,' says he, 'if it was not you, it was your father, and that is all one.' —So he seized the poor, innocent, helpless

thing, tore it to pieces, and made a meal
of it.

APPLICATION.

The thing which is pointed at in this fable
is so obvious, that it will be impertinent to
multiply words about it. When a cruel ill-
natured man has a mind to abuse one inferior
to himself, either in power or courage, though
he has not given the least occasion for it, how
does he resemble the Wolf! whose envious,
rapacious temper could not bear to see innocence live quietly in its neighbourhood. In
short, wherever ill people are in power, innocence and integrity are sure to be persecuted:
the more vicious the community is, the better
countenance they have for their own villanous
measures. To practise honesty in bad times,
is being liable to suspicion enough; but if any
one should dare to prescribe it, it is ten to one

but he would be impeached of high crimes and misdemeanors: for to stand up for justice in a degenerate and corrupt state, is tacitly to upbraid the government, and seldom fails of pulling down vengeance upon the head of him that offers to stir in its defence. Where cruelty and malice are in combination with power, nothing is so easy as for them to find a pretence to tyrannize over innocence, and exercise all manner of injustice.

FABLE III.

THE LION AND THE FOUR BULLS.

Four Bulls, which had entered into a very strict friendship, kept always near one another, and fed together. The Lion often saw them, and as often had a mind to makeone of them his prey; but, though he could easily have subdued any of them singly, yet he was afraid to attack the whole alliance, as knowing they would have been too hard for him, and therefore contented himself, for the present, with keeping at a distance. At last, perceiving no attempt was to be made upon them as long as this combination held, he took occasion, by whispers and hints, to foment jealousies, and raise divisions among them. This stratagem succeeded so well, that the Bulls grew cold and reserved towards one another, which soon after ripened into a downright hatred and aversion: and, at last, ended in a total separation. The Lion had now obtained his ends; and, as impossible as it was for him to hurt them while they were united, he found no difficulty, now they were parted, to seize and devour every Bull of them, one after another.

APPLICATION.

The moral of this fable is so well known and allowed, that to go about to enlighten it, would be like holding a candle to the sun. "A kingdom divided against itself cannot stand;" and as undisputed a maxim as it is, was, however thought necessary to be urged to the attention of mankind, by the best man that ever lived. And since friendships and alliances are of so great importance to our well-being and happiness, we cannot be too often cautioned not to let them be broken by tale-bearers and whisperers, or any other contrivance of our enemies.

13

FABLE IV.

THE FROG AND THE FOX.

A Frog, leaping out of the lake, and taking the advantage of a rising ground, made proclamation to all the beasts of the forest, that he was an able physician, and, for curing all manner of distempers, would turn his back to no person living. This discourse, uttered in a parcel of hard, cramp words, which nobody understood, made the beasts admire his learning, and give credit to every thing he said. At last the Fox, who was present, with indigna-

tion asked him, how he could have the impudence, with those thin lantern-jaws, that
meagre pale phyz, and blotched spotted body,
to set up for one who was able to cure the
infirmities of others.

APPLICATION.

A sickly, infirm look, is as disadvantageous
in a physician, as that of a rake in a clergy-
man, or a sheepish one in a soldier. If this
moral contains any thing further, it is, that we
should not set up for rectifying enormities in
others, while we labour under the same ourselves. Good advice ought always to be followed, without our being prejudiced upon account of the person from whom it comes: but
it is seldom that men can be brought to think
us worth minding, when we prescribe cures
for maladies with which ourselves are infected.
" Physician, heal thyself," is too scriptural not

to be applied upon such an occasion; and, if we would avoid being the jest of an audience, we must be sound, and free from those diseases of which we would endeavour to cure others. How shocked must people have been to hear a preacher, for a whole hour, declaim against drunkenness, when his own infirmity has been such, that he could neither bear nor forbear drinking; and, perhaps, was the only person in the congregation who made the doctrine at that time necessary! Others too have been very zealous in exploding crimes, for which none were more suspected than themselves: but let such silly hypocrites remember, that they whose eyes want couching, are the most improper people in the world to set up for oculists.

FABLE V.

THE ASS EATING THISTLES.

An Ass was loaded with good provisions of
several sorts, which, in time of harvest, he was
carrying into the field for his master and the
reapers to dine upon. By the way he met with
a fine large Thistle, and, being very hungry,
began to mumble it; which, while he was
doing, he entered into this reflection—'How
many greedy epicures would think themselves
happy, amidst such a variety of delicate viands
as I now carry! But to me, this bitter prickly

Thistle is more savoury and relishing than the most exquisite and sumptuous banquet.

Happiness and misery, and oftentimes pleasure and pain, exist merely in our opinion, and are no more to be accounted for than the difference of tastes. " That which is one man's meat, is another man's poison," is a proposition that ought to be allowed in all particulars, where the opinion is concerned, as well as in eating and drinking. Our senses must inform us whether a thing pleases or displeases, before we can declare our judgment of it ; and that is to any man good or evil, which his own understanding suggests to him to be so, and not that which is agreeable to another's fancy. And yet, as reasonable and as necessary as it is to grant this, how apt are we to wonder at people for not liking this or that, or how can they think so and so! This childish humour of wondering at the different tastes and opinions of others, occasions much uneasiness among the generality of mankind. But, if we considered things rightly, why should we be more concerned at others differing from us in their way of thinking upon any subject whatever, than at their liking cheese, or mustard; one, or both of which, we may happen to dislike? In truth, he that expects all mankind should be of his opinion, is much more stupid and unreasonable than the Ass in the fable.

FABLE VÌ.

THE LARK AND HER YOUNG ONES.

A LARK, who had Young Ones in a field of corn which was almost ripe, was under some fear lest the reapers should come to reap it before her young brood were fledged, and able to remove from the place; wherefore, upon flying abroad to look for food, she left this charge with them—that they should take notice what they heard talked of in her absence, and tell her of it when she came back again. When she was gone, they heard the owner of the corn call to his son—'Well,' says he, 'I think this corn is ripe enough; I would have you go early to-morrow, and desire our friends and neighbours to come and help us to reap it.' When the Old Lark came home, the Young Ones fell a quivering and chirping round her, and told her what had happened, begging her to remove them as fast as she could. The mother bid them be easy; 'for,' says she, 'if the owner depends upon friends and neighbours, I am pretty sure the corn will not be reaped to morrow.' Next day she went out again, upon the same occasion, and left the same orders with them as before. The owner came, and stayed, expecting those he had sent to: but the sun grew hot, and nothing was done, for not a soul came to help him. 'Then,' says he to his son, 'I perceive these friends of ours are not to be depended upon; so that you must even go to your uncles and cousins, and tell them, I desire they would be here betimes to-morrow morning to help us to reap.' Well, this the Young Ones, in a great fright, reported also to their mother. ' If that be all,' says she, ' do not be frightened, children, for kindred and relations do not use to be so very forward to serve one another: but take particular notice what you hear said the next time, and be sure you let me know it.' She went abroad the next day, as usual; and the owner, finding his relations as slack as the rest of his neighbours, said to his son, ' Harkye, George, do you get a couple of good sickles ready against to-morrow morning, and we will even reap the corn ourselves.' When the Young Ones told their mother this, 'Then,' says she, ' we must be gone indeed; for, when a man undertakes to do his business himself, it is not so, likely that he will be disappointed.' So she removed her Young Ones immediately, and the corn was reaped the next day by the good man and his son.

APPLICATION.

Never depend upon the assistance of friends and relations in any thing which you are able to do yourself; for nothing is more fickle and uncertain. The man, who relies upon another for the execution of any affair of importance, is not only kept in a wretched and slavish suspense while he expects the issue of the matter, but generally meets with a disappointment. While he, who lays the chief stress of his business upon himself, and depends upon his own industry and attention for the success of his affairs, is in the fairest way to attain his end: and, if at last he should miscarry, has this to comfort him—that it was not through his own negligence, and a vain expectation of the assistance of friends. To stand by ourselves, as much as possible, to exert our own strength and vigilance in the prosecution of our affairs, is godlike, being the result of a most noble and highly exalted reason ; but they who procrastinate and defer the business of life by an idle dependance upon others, in things which it is in their own power to effect, sink down into a kind of stupid abject slavery, and shew themselves unworthy of the talents with which human nature is dignified.

FABLE VII.

THE COCK AND THE FOX.

THE Fox, passing early one summer's morning near a farm-yard, was caught in a springe, which the farmer had planted there for that end. The Cock, at a distance, saw what happened; and, hardly yet daring to trust himself too near so dangerous a foe, approached him cautiously, and peeped at him, not without some horror and dread of mind. Reynard no sooner perceived it, but he addressed himself to him, with all the designing artifice imaginable. ' Dear cousin,' says he, ' you see what an unfortunate accident has befallen me here, and all upon your account: for, as I was creeping through yonder hedge, in my way homeward, I heard you crow, and was resolved to ask you how you did before I went any further: but, by the way, I met with this disaster; and therefore now I must become an humble suitor to you for a knife to cut this plaguy string; or, at least, that you would conceal my misfortune, till I have gnawed it asunder with my teeth.' The Cock, seeing how the case stood, made no reply, but posted away as fast as he could, and gave the farmer an account of the whole matter; who, taking a good weapon along with him, came and did the Fox's business, before he could have time to contrive his escape.

APPLICATION.

Though there is no quality of the mind more graceful in itself, or that renders it more amiable to others, than the having a tender regard to those who are in distress; yet we may err, even in this point, unless we take care to let our compassion flow out upon proper objects only. When the innocent fall into misfortune, it is the part of a generous brave spirit to contribute to their redemption; or, if that be impossible, to administer something to their comfort and support. But when wicked men, who have been enemies to their fellow-subjects, are entrapped in their own pernicious schemes, he that labours to deliver them, makes himself an associate in their crimes, and becomes as great an enemy to the public as those whom he would screen and protect.

When highwaymen and housebreakers are taken, condemned, and going to satisfy justice, at the expense of their vile paltry lives; who are they that grieve for them, and would be glad to rescue them from the rope? Not honest men, we may be sure. The rest of the thieving fraternity would, perhaps, commiserate their condition, and be ready to mutiny in their favour: nay, the rascally solicitor, who had been employed upon their account, would be vexed that his negotiations had succeeded no better, and be afraid of losing his reputation among other delinquents for the future; but every friend to justice would have no reason to be dissatisfied at any thing but a mournful reflection, which he could not forbear making, that, while these little criminals swing for some trifling inconsiderable rapine, others, so transcendently their superiors in fraud and plunder, escape with a whole skin.

FABLE VIII.

THE FOX IN THE WELL.

A Fox having fallen into a Well, made a shift, by sticking his claws into the sides, to keep his head above water. Soon after, a Wolf came and peeped over the brink; to whom the Fox applied himself very earnestly for assistance; entreating that he would help him to a rope, or something of that kind, which might favour his escape. The Wolf, moved with compassion at his misfortune, could not forbear expressing his concern: ' Ah! poor Reynard,' says he, ' I am sorry for you with all my heart; how could you possibly come into this melancholy condition?'— 'Nay, pr'ythee, friend,' replies the Fox, 'if you wish me well, do not stand pitying of me, but lend me some succour as fast as you can: for pity is but cold comfort when one is up to the chin in water, and within a hair's breadth of starving or drowning.'

APPLICATION.

Pity, indeed, is of itself but poor comfort at any time; and, unless it produces something more substantial, is rather impertinently troublesome, than any way agreeable. To stand bemoaning the misfortunes of our friends, without offering some expedient to alleviate them, is only echoing to their grief, and puting them in mind that they are miserable. He is truly my friend who, with a ready presence of mind, supports me; not he who condoles with me upon my ill success, and says he is sorry for my loss. In short, a favour or obligation is doubled by being well-timed; and he is the best benefactor, who knows our necessities, and complies with our wishes, even before we ask him.

35

FABLE IX.

THE WOLVES AND THE SHEEP.

THE Wolves and the Sheep had been a long time in a state of war together. At last a cessation of arms was proposed, in order to a treaty of peace, and hostages were to be delivered on both sides for security. The Wolves proposed that the Sheep should give up their dogs, on the one side, and that they would deliver up their young ones, on the other. This proposal was agreed to; but no sooner executed, than the young Wolves began to howl

for want of their dams. The old ones took
this opportunity to cry out, the treaty was
broke; and so falling upon the Sheep, who
were destitute of their faithful guardians the
dogs, they worried and devoured them without controul.

APPLICATION.

In all our transactions with mankind, even
in the most private and low life, we should
have a special regard how, and with whom, we
trust ourselves. Men, in this respect, ought to
look upon each other as Wolves, and to keep
themselves under a secure guard, and in a continual posture of defence. Particularly upon
any treaties of importance, the securities on
both sides should be strictly considered ; and
each should act with so cautious a view to their
own interest, as never to pledge or part with
that which is the very essence and basis of their

safety and well-being. And if this be a just
and reasonable rule for men to govern themselves by, in their own private affairs, how
much more fitting and necessary is it in any
conjuncture wherein the public is concerned?
If the enemy should demand our whole army
for an hostage, the danger in our complying
with it would be so gross and apparent, that
we could not help observing it: but, perhaps,
a country may equally expose itself by parting
with a particular town or general, as its whole
army; its safety, not seldom, depending as
much upon one of the former, as upon the
latter. In short, hostages and securities may
be something very dear to us, but ought never
to be given up, if our welfare and preservation
have any dependance upon them.

FABLE X.

THE EAGLE AND THE FOX.

An Eagle that had young ones, looking out for something to feed them with, happened to spy a Fox's cub, that lay basking itself abroad in the sun. She made a stoop, and trussed it immediately; but before she had carried it quite off, the old Fox coming home, implored her, with tears in her eyes, to spare her cub, and pity the distress of a poor fond mother, who should think no affliction so great as that of losing her child. The Eagle, whose nest was up in a very high tree, thought herself secure enough from all projects of revenge, and so bore away the cub to her young ones, without shewing any regard to the supplications of the Fox. But that subtle creature, highly incensed at this outrageous barbarity, ran to an altar, where some country people had been sacrificing a kid in the open fields, and catching up a firebrand in her mouth, made towards the tree where the Eagle's nest was, with a resolution of revenge. She had scarce ascended the first branches, when the Eagle, terrified with the approaching ruin of herself and family, begged of the Fox to desist, and with much submission, returned her the cub again safe and sound.

APPLICATION.

This fable is a warning to us not to deal hardly or injuriously by any body. The consideration of our being in a high condition of

life, and those we hurt, far below us, will plead
little or no excuse for us in this case: for there
is scarce a creature of so despicable a rank, but
is capable of avenging itself some way and at
some time or other. When great men happen
to be wicked, how little scruple do they make
of oppressing their poor neighbours! They are
perched upon a lofty station, and have built
their nest on nigh; and, having outgrown all
feelings of humanity, are insensible of any
pangs of remorse. The widow's tears, the or-
phan's cries, and the curses of the miserable,
like javelins thrown by the hand of a feeble
old man, fall by the way, and never reach their
heart. But let such a one, in the midst of his
flagrant injustice, remember, how easy a matter
it is, notwithstanding his superior distance, for
the meanest vassal to be revenged of him. The
bitterness of an affliction, even where cunning
is wanting, may animate the poorest spirit with

resolutions of vengeance; and, when once that fury is thoroughly awakened, we know not what she will require before she is lulled to rest again. The most powerful tyrants cannot prevent a resolved assassination; there are a thousand different ways for any private man to do the business, who is heartily disposed to it, and willing to satisfy his appetite for revenge, at the expence of his life. An old woman may clap a firebrand in the palace of a prince, and it is in the power of a poor weak fool to destroy the children of the mighty.

43

FABLE XI.

THE WOLF IN SHEEP'S CLOTHING.

A Wolf, clothing himself in the skin of a Sheep, and getting in among the flock, by this means took the opportunity to devour many of them. At last the shepherd discovered him, and cunningly fastening a rope about his neck, tied him up to a tree which stood hard by. Some other shepherds happening to pass that way, and observing what he was about, drew near, and expressed their admiration at it. ' What,' says one of them, ' brother, do you make hanging of Sheep?'—' No,' replies the other, ' but I make hanging of a Wolf whenever I catch him, though in the habit and garb of a Sheep.' Then he shewed them their mistake, and they applauded the justice of the execution.

APPLICATION.

This fable shews us, that no regard is to be had to the mere habit or outside of any person, but to undisguised worth and intrinsic virtue. When we place our esteem upon the external garb, before we inform ourselves of the qualities which it covers, we may often mistake evil for good, and, instead of a Sheep, take a Wolf into our protection. Therefore, however innocent or sanctified any one may appear, as to the vesture wherewith he is clothed, we may act rashly, because we may be imposed upon, if from thence we take it for granted, that he is inwardly as good and righteous as his outward robe would persuade us he is. Men of judgment and penetration do not use to give an implicit credit to a particular habit, or a peculiar colour, but love to make a more exact scrutiny; for he that will not come up to the character of an honest, good kind of man, when stripped of his Sheep's Clothing, is but the more detestable for his intended imposture; as the Wolf was but the more obnoxious to the shepherd's resentment, by wearing a habit so little suiting with his manners.

FABLE XII.

THE FOWLER AND THE RINGDOVE.

A Fowler took his gun, and went into the woods a shooting. He spied a Ringdove among the branches of an oak, and intended to kill it. He clapped the piece to his shoulder, and took his aim accordingly. But, just as he was going to pull the trigger, an adder, which he had trod upon under the grass, stung him so painfully in the leg, that he was forced to quit his design, and threw his gun down in a passion. The poison immediately infected his blood, and his whole body began to mortify; which, when he perceived, he could not help owning it to be just. ' Fate,' says he, ' has brought destruction upon me while I was contriving the death of another.'

APPLICATION.

This is another lesson against injustice; a topic in which our just Author abounds. And, if we consider the matter fairly, we must allow it to be as reasonable that some one should do violence to us, as we should commit it upon another. When we are impartial in our reflections, thus we must always think. The unjust man, with a hardened unfeeling heart, can do a thousand bitter things to others: but if a single calamity touches himself, oh, how tender he is! How insupportable is the uneasiness it occasions! Why should we think others born to hard treatment more than ourselves?

Or imagine it can be reasonable to do to another, what we ourselves should be unwilling to suffer? In our behaviour to all mankind, we need only ask ourselves these plain questions, and our consciences will tell us how to act. Conscience, like a good valuable domestic, plays the remembrancer to us upon all occasions, and gives us a gentle twitch, when we are going to do a wrong thing. It does not, like the adder in the fable, bite us to death, but only gives us kind cautions. However, if we neglect these just and frequent warnings, and continue in a course of wickedness and injustice, do not let us be surprised if Providence thinks fit, at last, to give us a home sting, and to exercise a little retaliation upon us.

FABLE XIII.

THE SOW AND THE WOLF.

A Sow had just farrowed, and lay in the stye, with her whole litter of pigs about her. A Wolf, who longed for one of them, but knew not how to come at it, endeavoured to insinuate himself into the Sow's good opinion: and, accordingly, coming up to her—'How does the good woman in the straw do?' says he. 'Can I be of any service to you, Mrs. Sow, in relation to your little family here? If you have a mind to go abroad, and air yourself a little, or so, you may depend upon it, I will take as much care of your pigs as you could do yourself.'—' Your humble servant,' says the Sow, ' I thoroughly understand your meaning; and, to let you know I do, I must be so free as to tell you, I had rather have your room than your company; and, therefore, if you would act like a Wolf of honour, and oblige me, I beg I may never see your face again.'

APPLICATION.

The being officiously good-natured and civil is something so uncommon in the world, that one cannot hear a man make profession of it without being surprised, or, at least, suspecting the disinterestedness of his intentions. Especially, when one who is a stranger to us, or, though known, is ill-esteemed by us, will be making offers of services, we have great reason to look to ourselves, and exert a shyness and coldness towards him. We should resolve not to receive even favours from bad kind of people; for should it happen that some immediate mischief was not couched in them, yet it is dangerous to have obligations to such, or to give them an opportunity of making a communication with us.

FABLE XVI.

THE HORSE AND THE ASS.

THE Horse, adorned with his great war saddle, and champing his foaming bridle, came thundering along the way, and made the mountains echo with his loud shrill neighing. He had not gone far, before he overtook an Ass, who was labouring under a heavy burden, and moving slowly on in the same track with himself. Immediately he called out to him, in a haughty imperious tone, and threatened to trample him in the dirt, if he did not break the way for him. The poor patient Ass, not daring to dispute the matter, quietly got out of his way as fast as he could, and let him go by. Not long after this, the same Horse, in an engagement with the enemy, happened to be shot in the eye, which made him unfit for shew, or any military business; so he was stript of his fine ornaments, and sold to a carrier. The Ass, meeting him in this forlorn condition, thought that now it was his time to insult; and so, says he, ' Hey-day, friend, is it you? Well, I always believed that pride of yours would one day have a fall.'

APPLICATION.

Pride is a very unaccountable vice: many people fall into it unawares, and are often led into it by motives, which, if they considered things rightly, would make them abhor the very thoughts of it. There is no man that thinks well of himself, but desires that the rest of the world should think so too. Now it is the wrong measures we take in endeavouring after this, that expose us to discerning people in that light which they call pride, and which is so far from giving us any advantage in their esteem, that it renders us despicable and ridiculous. It is an affectation of appearing considerable that puts men upon being proud and insolent; and their very being so makes them, infallibly, little and inconsiderable. The man that claims and calls for reverence and respect, deserves none; he that asks for applause, is sure to lose it: the certain way to get it is to seem to shun it; and the humble man, according to the maxims even of this world, is the most likely to be exalted. He that, in his words or actions, pleads for superiority, and rather chooses to do an ill action, than condescend to do a good one, acts like a Horse, and is as void of reason and understanding. The rich and the powerful want nothing but the love and esteem of mankind to complete their felicity; and these they are sure to obtain by a good-humoured, kind condescension; and as certain of being every body's aversion, while the least tincture of overbearing rudeness is perceptible in their words or actions. What brutal tempers must they be of, who can be easy and indifferent, while they know themselves to be universally hated, though in the midst of affluence and power! But this is not all; for if ever the wheel of fortune should whirl them from the top to the bottom, instead of friendship or commiseration, they will meet with nothing but contempt; and that with much more justice than ever they themselves exerted it towards others.

FABLE XV.

THE WOLF, THE LAMB, AND THE GOAT.

A Wolf, meeting a Lamb, one day, in company with a Goat—' Child,' says he, ' you are mistaken; this is none of your mother; she is yonder; pointing to a flock of sheep at a distance.—' It may be so,' says the Lamb; ' the person that happened to conceive me, and afterwards bore me a few months in her belly because she could not help it, and then dropt me, she did not care where, and left me to the wide world, is, I suppose, what you call my mother; but I look upon this charitable Goat as such, that took compassion on me in my poor, helpless, destitute condition, and gave me suck; sparing it out of the mouths of her own kids, rather than I should want it.—' But sure,' says he, ' you have a greater regard for her that gave you life, than for any body else.'— ' She gave me life! I deny that. She that could not so much as tell whether I should be black or white, had a great hand in giving me life, to be sure! But, supposing it were so, I am mightily obliged to her, truly, for contriving to let me be of the male-kind, so that I go every day in danger of the butcher. What reason then have I to have a greater regard for one to whom I am so little indebted for any part of my being, than for those from whom I have received all the benevolence and kindness which have hitherto supported me in life?'

APPLICATION.

It is they whose goodness makes them our parents, that properly claim our filial respect from us, and not those who are such only out of necessity. The duties between parents and their children are relative and reciprocal. By all laws, natural as well as civil, it is expected that the parents should cherish and provide for the child, till it is able to shift for itself; and that the child, with a mutual tenderness, should depend upon the parent for its sustenance, and yield it a reasonable obedience. Yet, through the depravity of human nature, we very often see these laws violated, and the relations before mentioned treating one another with as much virulence as enemies of different countries are capable of. Through the natural impatience and protervity of youth, we observe the first occasion for any animosity most frequently arising from their side; but, however, there are not wanting examples of undutiful parents: and, when a father, by using a son ill, and denying him such an education and such an allowance as his circumstances can well afford, gives him occasion to withdraw his respect from him, to urge his begetting of him as the sole obligation to duty, is talking like a silly, unthinking dotard. Mutual benevolence must be kept up between relations, as well as friends; for, without this cement, whatever you please to call the building, it is only a castle in the air, a thing to be talked of, without the least reality.

63

FABLE XVI.

THE KITE AND THE PIGEONS.

A Kite, who had kept sailing in the air for many days near a dove-house, and made a stoop at several Pigeons, but all to no purpose, (for they were too nimble for him) at last had recourse to stratagem, and took his opportunity one day to make a declaration to them, in which he set forth his own just and good intentions, who had nothing more at heart than the defence and protection of the Pigeons in their ancient rights and liberties, and how con-

cerned he was at their fears and jealousies of a
foreign invasion, especially their unjust and
unreasonable suspicions of himself, as if he
intended, by force of arms, to break in upon
their constitution, and erect a tyrannical government over them. To prevent all which,
and thoroughly to quiet their minds, he thought
proper to propose to them such terms of alliance and articles of peace as might for ever
cement a good understanding betwixt them:
the principal of which was, that they should
accept of him for their king, and invest him
with all kingly privilege and prerogative over
them. The poor simple Pigeons consented:
the Kite took the coronation oath after a very
solemn manner, on his part, and the Doves,
the oaths of allegiance and fidelity, on theirs.
But much time had not passed over their heads,
before the good Kite pretended that it was part
of his prerogative to devour a Pigeon when-

ever he pleased. And this he was not contented to do himself only, but instructed the
rest of the royal family in the same kingly
arts of government. The Pigeons, reduced to
this miserable condition, said one to the other,
' Ah! we deserve no better! Why did we let
him come in?'

APPLICATION.

What can this fable be applied to but the
exceeding blindness and stupidity of that part
of mankind who wantonly and foolishly trust
their native rights of liberty without good
security? Who often choose for guardians of
their lives and fortunes, persons abandoned to
the most unsociable vices; and seldom have
any better excuse for such an error in politics
than, that they were deceived in their expectation; or never thoroughly knew the manners
of their king till he had got them entirely in

his power: which, however, is notoriously false: for many, with the Doves in the fable, are so silly, that they would admit of a Kite, rather than be without a king. The truth is, we ought not to incur the possibility of being deceived in so important a matter as this: an unlimited power should not be trusted in the hands of any one who is not endued with a perfection more than human.

67

FABLE XVII.

λ

THE COUNTRY MOUSE AND THE CITY MOUSE.

An honest, plain, sensible Country Mouse is said to have entertained at his hole one day a fine Mouse of the Town. Having formerly been playfellows together, they were old acquaintance, which served as an apology for the visit. However, as master of the house, he thought himself obliged to do the honours of it, in all respects, and to make as great a stranger of his guest as he possibly could. In order to this, he set before him a reserve of de-

licate grey peas and bacon, a dish of fine oat-
meal, some parings of new cheese, and, to
crown all with a desert, a remnant of a charming mellow apple. In good manners, he for-
bore to eat any himself, lest the stranger should
not have enough; but, that he might seem to
bear the other company, sat and nibbled a
piece of a wheaten straw very busily. At last
says the spark of the town, ' Old crony, give me
leave to be a little free with you; how can you
bear to live in this nasty, dirty, melancholy hole
here, with nothing but woods, and meadows,
and mountains, and rivulets, about you? Do
not you prefer the conversation of the world
to the chirping of birds, and the splendor of a
court to the rude aspect of an uncultivated
desert? Come, take my word for it, you will
find it a change for the better. Never stand
considering, but away this moment. Remember, we are not immortal, and therefore have

no time to lose. Make sure of to-day, and spend it as agreeably as you can; you know not what may happen to-morrow.' In short, these and such like arguments prevailed, and his Country Acquaintance was resolved to go to town that night. So they both set out upon their journey together, proposing to sneak in after the close of the evening. They did so; and, about midnight, made their entry into a certain great house, where there had been an extraordinary entertainment the day before, and several tit-bits, which some of the servants had purloined, were hid under the seat of a window. The Country Guest was immediately placed in the midst of a rich Persian carpet: and now it was the Courtier's turn to entertain; who, indeed, acquitted himself in that capacity with the utmost readiness and address, changing the courses as elegantly, and tasting every thing first as judiciously, as any clerk of a kitchen. The other sat and enjoyed himself like a delighted epicure, tickled to the last degree with this new turn of his affairs; when, on a sudden, a noise of somebody opening the door made them start from their seats, and scuttle in confusion about the dining-room. Our Country Friend, in particular, was ready to die with fear at the barking of a huge mastiff or two, which opened their throats just about the same time, and made the whole house echo. At last, recovering himself,—' Well,' says he, ' if this be your town life, much good may do you with it: give me my poor quiet hole again, with my homely, but comfortable, grey peas.'

APPLICATION.

A moderate fortune, with a quiet retirement in the country, is preferable to the greatest affluence which is attended with care and the perplexity of business, and inseparable from the noise and hurry of the town. The practice of the generality of people of the best taste, it is to be owned, is directly against us in this point; but, when it is considered that this practice of theirs proceeds rather from a compliance with the fashion of the times, than their own private thoughts, the objection is of no force. Among the great numbers of men who have received a learned education, how few are there but either have their fortunes entirely to make, or, at least, think they deserve to have, and ought not to lose the opportunity of geting, somewhat more than their fathers have left them! The town is the field of action for volunteers of this kind; and whatever fondness they may have for the country, yet they must stay till their circumstances will admit of a retreat thither. But sure there never was a man yet, who lived in a constant return of trouble and fatigue in town, as all men of busi-

ness do in some degree or other, but has formed
to himself some end of getting some sufficient
competency, which may enable him to purchase a quiet possession in the country, where
he may indulge his genius, and give up his old
age to that easy smooth life which, in the tempest of business, he had so often longed for.
Can any thing argue more strongly for a country life, than to observe what a long course of
labour people go through, and what difficulties
they encounter, to come at it? They look upon
it, at a distance, like a kind of heaven, a place
of rest and happiness; and are pushing forward
through the rugged thorny cares of the world,
to make their way towards it. If there are
many who, though born to plentiful fortunes,
yet live most part of their time in the noise, the
smoke, and hurry of the town, we shall find,
upon inquiry, that necessary indispensable business is the real or pretended plea which most

of them have to make for it. The court and the senate require the attendance of some: law-suits, and the proper direction of trade, engage others: they who have a sprightly wit and an elegant taste for conversation, will resort to the place which is frequented by people of the same turn, whatever aversion they may otherwise have for it; and others, who have no such pretence, have yet this to say, that they follow the fashion. They who appear to have been men of the best sense amongst the ancients, always recommended the country as the most proper scene for innocence, ease, and virtuous pleasure, and, accordingly, lost no opportunities of enjoying it: and men of the greatest distinction among the moderns, have ever thought themselves most happy when they could be decently spared from the employments which the excellency of their talents necessarily threw them into, to embrace the charming leisure of a country life.

FABLE XVIII.

THE SWALLOW AND OTHER BIRDS.

A FARMER was sowing his field with flax. The Swallow observed it, and desired the other Birds to assist her in picking the seed up, and destroying it; telling them, that flax was that pernicious material of which the thread was composed which made the fowler's nets, and by that means contributed to the ruin of so many innocent Birds. But the poor Swallow not having the good fortune to be regarded, the flax sprung up, and appeared above the ground. She then put them in mind once more of their impending danger, and wished them to pluck it up in the bud, before it went any farther. They still neglected her warnings; and the flax grew up into the high stalk. She yet again desired them to attack it, for that it was not yet too late. But all that she could get was to be ridiculed and despised for a silly pretending prophet. The Swallow finding all her remonstrances availed nothing, was resolved to leave the society of such unthinking, careless creatures, before it was too late. So quitting the woods, she repaired to the houses, and forsaking the conversation of the Birds, has ever since made her abode among the dwellings of men.

APPLICATION.

As men, we should always exercise so much humanity as to endeavour the welfare of man-

kind, particularly of our acquaintance and relations; and, if by nothing farther, at least by
our good advice. When we have done this,
and, if occasion required, continued to repeat it
a second or third time, we shall have acquitted
ourselves sufficiently from any imputation upon
their miscarriage; and having nothing more to
do but to separate ourselves from them, that
we may not be involved in their ruin, or be
supposed to partake of their error. This is an
excommunication which reason allows. For
as it would be cruel, on the one side, to prose-
cute and hurt people for being mistaken, so,
on the other, it would be indiscreet and over
complaisant, to keep them company through
all their wrong notions, and act contrary to our
opinion out of pure civility

...md...r, sculp,

FABLE XIX.

THE HUNTED BEAVER.

It is said that a Beaver (a creature which lives chiefly in the water) has a certain part about him which is good in physic, and that, upon this account, he is often hunted down and killed. Once upon a time, as one of these creatures was hard pursued by the dogs, and knew not how to escape, recollecting with himself the reason of his being thus persecuted, with a great resolution and presence of mind he bit off the part which his hunters wanted, and throwing it towards them, by these means ecsaped with his life.

APPLICATION.

However it is amongst beasts, there are few human creatures but what are hunted for something else besides either their lives or the pleasure of hunting them. The inquisition would hardly be so keen against the Jews, if they had not something belonging to them which their persecutors esteem more valuable than their souls; which whenever that wise, but obstinate people, can prevail with themselves to part with, there is an end of the chase for that time. Indeed, when life is pursued, and in danger, whoever values it, should give up every thing but his honour to preserve it. And when a discarded minister is prosecuted for having damaged the common-wealth, let him but throw down some of the fruits of his iniquity to the hunters, and one may engage for his coming off, in other respects, with a whole skin.

81

FABLE XX.

THE CAT AND THE FOX.

As the Cat and the Fox were talking politics together, on a time, in the middle of a forest, Reynard said, ' Let things turn out ever so bad, he did not care, for he had a thousand tricks for them yet, before they should hurt him.'—' But pray,' says he, ' Mrs. Puss, suppose there should be an invasion, what course do you design to take!'—' Nay,' says the Cat, ' I have but one shift for it, and if that won't do, I am undone.' —' I am sorry for you,' replies Reynard, ' with all my heart, and would gladly furnish you

with one or two of mine, but indeed, neighbour, as times go, it is not good to trust; we
must even be every one for himself, as the saying is, and so your humble servant.' These
words were scarce out of his mouth, when
they were alarmed with a pack of hounds,
that came upon them full cry. The Cat, by
the help of her single shift, ran up a tree, and
sat securely among the top branches: from
whence she beheld Reynard, who had not been
able to get out of sight, overtaken with his
thousand tricks, and torn in as many pieces by
the dogs which had surrounded him.

APPLICATION.

A man that sets up for more cunning than
the rest of his neighbours is generally a silly
fellow at the bottom. Whoever is master of a
little judgment and insight into things, let
him keep them to himself, and make use of

them as he sees occasion; but he should not be teasing others with an idle and impertinent ostentation of them. One good discreet expedient, made use of upon an emergency, will do a man more real service, and make others think better of him, than to have passed all along for a shrewd crafty knave, and be bubbled at last. When any one has been such a coxcomb as to insult his acquaintance, by pretending to more policy and stratagem than the rest of mankind, they are apt to wish for some difficulty for him to shew his skill in; where, if he should miscarry, (as ten to one but he does) his misfortune, instead of pity, is sure to be attended with laughter. He that sets up for a biter, as the phrase is, being generally intent upon his prey, or vain of shewing his art, frequently exposes himself to the traps of one sharper than himself, and incurs the ridicule of those whom he designed to make ridiculous.

FABLE XXI.

THE CAT AND THE MICE.

A CERTAIN house was much infested with Mice; but at last they got a Cat, who catched and eat every day some of them. The Mice, finding their numbers grow thin, consulted what was best to be done for the preservation of the public from the jaws of the devouring Cat .They debated and came to this resolution, That no one should go down below the upper shelf. The Cat, observing the Mice no longer came down as usual, hungry and disappointed of her prey, had recourse to this stratagem; she hung by her hinder legs on a peg which stuck in the wall, and made as if she had been dead, hoping by this lure to entice the Mice to come down. She had not been in this posture long, before a cunning old Mouse peeped over the edge of the shelf, and spoke thus:— 'Aha, my good friend, are you there! there may you be! I would not trust myself with you, though your skin were stuffed with straw.'

APPLICATION.

Prudent folks never trust those a second time who have deceived them once. And, indeed, we cannot well be too cautious in following this rule: for, upon examination, we shall find, that most of the misfortunes which befall us, proceed from our too great credulity.

They that know how to suspect, without ex-
posing or hurting themselves, till honesty
comes to be more in fashion, can never suspect
too much.

FABLE XXII.

THE LION AND OTHER BEASTS.

THE Lion and several other beasts entered into an alliance offensive and defensive, and were to live very sociably together in the forest. One day, having made a sort of an excursion by way of hunting, they took a very fine, large, fat deer, which was divided into four parts; there happening to be then present his majesty the Lion, and only three others. After the division was made, and the parts were set out, his majesty advancing forward some steps,

and pointing to one of the shares, was pleased
to declare himself after the following manner:
' This I seize and take possession of as my
right, which devolves to me, as I am descended
by a true, lineal, hereditary succession from
the royal family of Lion: that (pointing to
the second) I claim by, I think, no unreasonable demand; considering that all the engage-
ments you have with the enemy turn chiefly
upon my courage and conduct; and you very
well know, that wars are too expensive to be
carried on without proper supplies. Then
(nodding his head towards the third) that I
shall take by virtue of my prerogative; to
which, I make no question, but so dutiful and
loyal a people will pay all the deference and
regard that I can desire. Now, as for the re-
maining part, the necessity of our present affairs is so very urgent, our stock so low, and
our credit so impaired and weakened, that I

must insist upon your granting that, without any hesitation or demur; and hereof fail not at your peril.'

APPLICATION.

No alliance is safe which is made with those that are superior to us in power. Though they lay themselves under the most strict and solemn ties at the opening of the congress, yet the first advantageous opportunity will tempt them to break the treaty; and they will never want specious pretences to furnish out their declarations of war. It is not easy to determine, whether it is more stupid and ridiculous for a community to trust itself first in the hands of those that are more powerful than themselves, or to wonder afterwards that their confidence and credulity are abused, and their properties invaded.

FABLE XXIII.

THE LION AND THE MOUSE.

A Lion, faint with heat, and weary with hunting, was laid down to take his repose under the spreading boughs of a thick shady oak. It happened that, while he slept, a company of scrambling mice ran over his back, and waked him: upon which, starting up, he clapped his paw upon one of them, and was just going to put it to death; when the little suppliant implored his mercy in a very moving manner, begging him not to stain his noble character with the blood of so despicable and small a beast. The Lion, considerng the matter, thought proper to do as he was desired, and immediately released his little trembling prisoner. Not long after, traversing the forest in pursuit of his prey, he chanced to run into the toils of the hunters; from whence, not able to disengage himself, he set up a most hideous and loud roar. The Mouse, hearing the voice, and knowing it to be the Lion's, immediately repaired to the place, and bid him fear nothing, for that he was his friend. Then straight he fell to work, and, with his little sharp teeth, gnawing asunder the knots and fastenings of the toils, set the royal brute at liberty.

APPLICATION.

This fable gives us to understand, that there is no person in the world so little, but even the greatest may, at some time or other, stand in need of his assistance; and consequently that it is good to use clemency, where there there is any room for it, towards those who fall within our power. A generosity of this kind is a handsome virtue, and looks very graceful whenever it is exerted, if there were nothing else in it: but as the lowest people in life may, upon occasion, have it in their power either to serve or hurt us, that makes it our duty, in point of common interest, to behave ourselves with good nature and lenity towards all with whom we have to do. Then the gratitude of the Mouse, and his readiness, not only to repay, but even to exceed, the obligation due to his benefactor, notwithstanding his little body, gives us the specimen of a great soul, which is never so much delighted as with an opportunity of shewing how sensible it is of favours received.

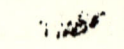

FABLE XXIV.

THE FATAL MARRIAGE.

The Lion aforesaid, touched with the grateful procedure of the Mouse, and resolving not to be outdone in generosity by any wild beast whatsoever, desired his little deliverer to name his own terms, for that he might depend upon his complying with any proposal he should make. The Mouse, fired with ambition at this gracious offer, did not so much consider what was proper for him to ask, as what was in the power of his prince to grant; and so presumptuously demanded his princely daughter, the young Lioness, in marriage. The Lion consented: but, when he would have given the royal virgin into his possession, she, like a giddy thing as she was, not minding how she walked, by chance set her paw upon her spouse, who was coming to meet her, and crushed her little dear to pieces.

APPLICATION.

This fable seems intended to shew us how miserable some people make themselves by a wrong choice, when they have all the good things in the world spread before them to choose out of. In short, if that one particular of judgment be wanting, it is not in the power of the greatest monarch upon earth, nor of the repeated smiles of fortune, to make us happy. It is the want or possession of a good judgment which oftentimes makes the prince a poor wretch, and the poor philosopher completely easy. Now, the first and chief degree of judgment is to know one's self; to be able to make a tolerable estimate of one's own capacity, so as not to speak or undertake any thing which may either injure or make us ridiculous: and yet (as wonderful as it is) there have been men of allowed good sense in particular, and possessed of all desirable qualifications in general, to make life delightful and agreeable, who have unhappily contrived to match themselves with women of a genius and temper necessarily tending to blast their peace. This proceeds from some unaccountable blindness: but when wealthy plebeians, of mean extraction and unrefined education, as an equivalent for their money, demand brides out of the nurseries of our peerage, their being despised, or at least overlooked, is so unavoidable, unless in extraordinary cases, that nothing but a false taste of glory could make them enter upon a scheme so inconsistent and unpromising.

FABLE XXV.

THE MISCHIEVOUS DOG.

A CERTAIN man had a Dog, which was so curst and mischievous, that he was forced to fasten a heavy clog about his neck, to keep him from running at and worrying people. This the vain cur took for a badge of honourable distinction; and grew so insolent upon it, that he looked down with an air of scorn upon the neighbouring dogs, and refused to keep them company. But a sly old poacher, who was one of the gang, assured him, that he had no reason to value himself upon the favour he wore, since it was fixed upon him rather as a mark of disgrace than of honour.

Some people are so exceeding vain, and at the same time so dull of apprehension, that they interpret every thing by which they are distinguished from others in their own favour. If they betray any weaknesses in conversation, which are apt to excite the laughter of their company, they make no scruple of ascribing it to their superiority in point of wit. If want of sense or breeding (one of which is always the case) disposes them to give, or mistake, affronts, upon which account all discreet sensible people are obliged to shun their company, they impute it to their own valour and magnanimity, to which they fancy the world pays an awful and respectful deference. There are several decent ways of pre venting such turbulent men from doing mischief, which might be applied with secrecy, and many times pass unregarded, if their own arrogance did not require the rest of mankind to take notice of it.

FABLE XXVI.

THE OX AND THE FROG.

An Ox, grazing in a meadow, chanced to set his foot among a parcel of young Frogs, and trod one of them to death. The rest informed their mother, when she came home, what had happened; telling her, that the beast which did it was the hugest creature that they ever saw in their lives. ' What, was it so big?' says the old Frog, swelling and blowing up her speckled belly to a great degree. ' Oh! bigger by a vast deal,' say they. ' And so big?' says she, straining herself yet more. ' Indeed, mamma,' say they, ' if you were to burst yourself, you would never be so big.' She strove yet again, and burst herself indeed.

APPLICATION.

Whenever a man endeavours to live equal with one of a greater fortune than himself, he is sure to share a like fate with the Frog in the fable. How many vain people, of moderate easy circumstances, burst and come to nothing, by vying with those whose estates are more ample than their own! Sir Changeling Plumstock was possessed of a very considerable estate, devolved to him by the death of an old uncle, who had adopted him his heir. He had a false taste of happiness; and, without the least economy, trusting to the sufficiency of his vast revenue, was resolved to be outdone by nobody in shewish grandeur and expensive living. He gave five thousand pounds for a piece of ground in the country to set a house upon; the building and furniture of which cost fifty thousand more; and his gardens were proportionably magnificent. Besides which, he thought himself under a necessity of buying out two or three tenements which stood in his neighbourhood, that he might have elbow-room enough. All this he could very well bear; and still might have been happy, had it not been for an unfortunate view which he one day happened to take of my Lord Castle-builder's gardens, which consist of twenty acres, whereas his own were not above twelve. From that time he grew pensive; and before the ensuing winter gave five and thirty years purchase for a dozen acres more to enlarge his gardens, built a couple of exorbitant green-houses, and a large pavilion at the farther end of a terrace-walk. The bare repairs and su-

perintendencies of all which call for the re-
maining part of his income.   He is mortgaged
pretty deep, and pays nobody; but, being a
privileged person, resides altogether at a private
cheap lodging in the city of Westminster.

behaviour towards our superiors: the one is a bashfulness, proceeding either from a vicious guilty mind, or a timorous rusticity; the other, an over-bearing impudence, which assumes more than becomes it, and so renders the person insufferable to the conversation of well-bred reasonable people. But there is this difference between the bashfulness that arises from a want of education, and the shame-facedness that accompanies conscious guilt; the first, by a continuance of time and a nearer acquaintance, may be ripened into a proper liberal behaviour; the other no sooner finds an easy practicable access, but it throws off all manner of reverence, grows every day more and more familiar, and branches out into the utmost indecency and irregularity. Indeed, there are many occasions which may happen to cast an awe, or even a terror, upon our minds at first view, without any just and reasonable grounds; but upon a little recollection, or a nearer insight, we recover ourselves, and can appear indifferent and unconcerned, where, before, we were ready to sink under a load of diffidence and fear. We should, upon such occasions, use our endeavours to regain a due degree of steadiness and resolution; but, at the same time, we must have a care that our efforts in that respect do not force the balance too much, and make it rise to an unbecoming freedom and an offensive familiarity.

FABLE XXVIII.

THE APE AND THE FOX.

THE Ape meeting the Fox one day, humbly requested him to give him a piece of his fine long brush tail, to cover his poor naked backside, which was exposed to all the violence and inclemency of the weather; 'For,' says he, 'Reynard, you have already more than you have occasion for, and a great part of it even drags along in the dirt.' The Fox answered, 'That as to his having too much, that was more than he knew; but be it as it would, he had rather sweep the ground with his tail as long as he lived, than deprive himself of the least bit to cover the Ape's nasty stinking posteriors.'

APPLICATION.

One cannot help considering the world, in the particular of the goods of fortune, as a kind of lottery; in which some few are entitled to prizes of different degrees; others, and those by much the greatest part, come off with little or nothing. Some, like the Fox, have even larger circumstances than they know what to do with, insomuch that they are rather a charge and incumbrance than of any true use and pleasure to them. Others, like the poor Ape's case, are all blank; not having been so lucky as to draw from the wheel of fortune wherewith to cover their nakedness, and live with tolerable decency. That these things are left in a great measure by Providence, to the blind uncertain shuffle of chance, is reasonable to conclude from the unequal distribution of them; for there is seldom any regard had to true merit upon these occasions; folly and knavery ride in coaches, while good sense and honesty walk in the dirt. The allwise Disposer of events does certainly permit these things for just and good purposes, which our shallow understanding is not able to fathom; but, humanly thinking, if the riches and power of the world were to be always in the hands of the virtuous part of mankind, they would be more likely to do good with them in their generation, than the vile sottish wretches who generally enjoy them. A truly good man would direct all the superfluous part of his wealth, at least, for the necessities of his fellow-creatures, though there were no religion which enjoined it: but selfish and avaricious people, who are always great knaves, how much soever they may have, will never think they have enough: much less be induced, by any consideration of virtue and religion, to part with the least farthing for public charity and beneficence.

FABLE XXIX.

THE DOG IN THE MANGER.

A Dog was lying upon a manger full of hay. An Ox, being hungry, came near, and offered to eat of the hay; but the envious ill-natured cur, getting up and snarling at him, would not suffer him to touch it. Upon which the Ox, in the bitterness of his heart, said, 'A curse light on thee, for a malicious wretch, who wilt neither eat hay thyself, nor suffer others to do it.'

APPLICATION.

Envy is the most unnatural and unaccountable of all the passions. There is scarce any
other emotion of the mind, however unreasonable, but may have something said in excuse
for it; and there are many of these weaknesses
of the soul, which, notwithstanding the wrong-
ness and irregularity of them, swell the heart,
while they last, with pleasure and gladness.
But the envious man has no such apology as
this to make; the stronger the passion is, the
greater torment he endures; and subjects himself to a continual real pain, by only wishing
ill to others. Revenge is sweet, though cruel
and inhuman; and though it sometimes thirsts
even for blood, yet may be glutted and sa-
tiated. Avarice is something highly monstrous
and absurd; yet, as it is a desire after riches,
every little acquisition gives it pleasure; and to
behold and feel the hoarded treasure, to a co-

vetous man, is a constant uncloying enjoyment. But envy, which is an anxiety arising in our minds, upon our observing accomplishments in others, which we want ourselves, can never receive any true comfort, unless in a deluge, a conflagration, a plague, or some general calamity that should befall mankind : for, as long as there is a creature living, that enjoys its being happily within the envious man's sphere, it will afford nourishment to his distempered mind; but such nourishment, as will make him pine, and fret, and emaciate himself to nothing.

FABLE XXX.

THE BIRDS, THE BEASTS, AND THE BAT.

ONCE upon a time there commenced a fierce
war between the Birds and the Beasts; when
the Bat, taking advantage of his ambiguous
make, hoped, by that means, to live secure in
a state of neutrality, and save his bacon. It
was not long before the forces on each side
met, and gave a battle; and, their animosities
running very high, a bloody slaughter ensued.
The Bat, at the beginning of the day, thinking the birds most likely to carry it, listed him-

self among them; but kept fluttering at a little distance, that he might the better observe, and take his measures accordingly. However, after some time spent in the action, the army of the Beasts, seeming to prevail, he went entirely over to them, and endeavoured to convince them, by the affinity which he had to a mouse, that he was by nature a beast, and would always continue firm and true to their interest. His plea was admitted; but, in the end, the advantage turning completely on the side of the Birds, under the admirable conduct and courage of their general the eagle, the Bat, to save his life, and escape the disgrace of falling into the hands of his deserted friends, betook himself to flight; and ever since, skulking in caves and hollow trees all day, as if ashamed to shew himself, he never appears till the dusk of the evening, when all the feathered inhabitants of the air are gone to roost.

APPLICATION.

For any one to desert the interest of his country, and turn renegado, either out of fear, or any prospect of advantage, is so notoriously vile and low, that it is no wonder if the man, who is detected in it, is for ever ashamed to see the sun, and to shew himself in the eyes of those whose cause he has betrayed. Yet, as there is scarce any vice, even to be imagined, but there may be found men who have been guilty of it, perhaps there have been as many criminals in the case before us, as in any one particular besides, notwithstanding the aggravation and extraordinary degree of its baseness. We cannot help reflecting upon it with horror: but, as truly detestable as this vice is, and must be acknowledged to be, by all mankind, so far are those that practise it from being treated with a just resentment by the rest of mankind, that by the kind reception they afterwards meet with, they rather seem to be encouraged and applauded, than despised and discountenanced, for it.

FABLE XXXI.

THE FOX AND THE TIGER.

A SKILFUL archer coming into the woods, directed his arrows so successfully, that he slew many wild beasts, and pursued several others. This put the whole savage kind into a fearful consternation, and made them fly to the most retired thickets for refuge. At last, the Tiger resumed a courage, and, bidding them not to be afraid, said, that he alone would engage the enemy; telling them, they might depend upon his valour and strength to revenge their wrongs. In the midst of these threats, while he was lashing himself with his tail, and tearing up the ground for anger, an arrow pierced his ribs, and hung by its barbed point in his side. He set up an hideous and loud roar, occasioned by the anguish which he felt, and endeavoured to draw out the painful dart with his teeth; when the Fox, approaching him, inquired with an air of surprise, who it was that could have strength and courage enough to wound so mighty and valorous a beast!—' Ah!' says the Tiger, ' I was mistaken in my reckoning: it was that invincible man yonder.'

APPLICATION.

Though strength and courage are very good ingredients towards the making us secure and formidable in the world, yet, unless there be a proper portion of wisdom or policy to direct them, instead of being serviceable, they often prove detrimental to their proprietors. A rash froward man, who depends upon the excellence of his own parts and accomplishments, is likewise apt to expose a weak side, which his enemies might not otherwise have observed, and gives an advantage to others by those very means which he fancied would have secured it to himself. Counsel and conduct always did, and always will, govern the world; and the strong, in spite of all their force, can never avoid being tools to the crafty. Some men are as much superior to others in wisdom and policy, as man, in general, is above a brute. Strength ill-concerted, opposed to them, is like a quarter-staff in the hands of a huge, robust, but bungling fellow, who fights against a master of the science. The latter, though without a weapon, would have skill and address enough to disarm his adversary, and drub him with his own staff. In a word, savage fierceness and brutal strength must not pretend to stand in competition with finesse and stratagem.

129

FABLE XXXII.

THE LIONESS AND THE FOX.

THE Lioness and the Fox meeting together fell into discourse; and the conversation turning upon the breeding and the fruitfulness of some living creatures above others, the Fox could not forbear taking the opportunity of observing to the Lioness, that, for her part, she thought Foxes were as happy in that respect as almost any other creatures; for that they bred constantly once a year, if not oftener, and always had a good litter of cubs at every birth:

'and yet,' says she, 'there are those who are never delivered of more than one at a time, and that perhaps not above once or twice through their whole life, who hold up their noses and value themselves so much upon it, that they think all other creatures beneath them, and scarce worthy to be spoken to.' The Lioness, who all the while perceived at whom this reflection pointed, was fired with resentment, and with a good deal of vehemence replied—' What you have observed may be true, and that not without reason. You produce a great many at a litter, and often; but what are they? Foxes. I indeed have but one at a time, but you should remember that this one is a Lion.'

APPLICATION.

Our productions, of whatsoever kind, are not to be esteemed so much by the quantity as the quality of them. It is not being employed much, but well, and to the purpose, which makes us useful to the age we live in, and celebrated by those which are to come. As it is a misfortune to the countries which are infested with them, for Foxes and other vermin to multiply; so, one cannot help throwing out a melancholy reflection, when one sees some particulars of the human kind increase so fast as they do. But the most obvious meaning of this fable is the hint it gives us in relation to authors. These gentlemen should never attempt to raise themselves a reputation, by enumerating a catalogue of their productions; since there is more glory in having written one tolerable piece than a thousand indifferent ones. And whoever has had the good fortune to please in one performance of this kind, should be very cautions how he ventures his reputation in a second.

FABLE XXXIII.

THE OAK AND THE REED.

An Oak, which hung over the bank of a river, was blown down by a violent storm of wind; and as it was carried along by the stream, some of its boughs brushed against a Reed which grew near the shore. This struck the Oak with a thought of admiration; and he could not forbear asking the Reed how he came to stand so secure and unhurt in a tempest, which had been furious enough to tear an Oak up by the roots? 'Why,' says the Reed, 'I secure myself by putting on a behaviour quite contrary to what you do; instead of being stubborn and stiff, and confiding in my strength, I yield and bend to the blast, and let it go over me; knowing how vain and fruitless it would be to resist.'

APPLICATION.

Though a tame submission to injuries which it is in our power to redress be generally esteemed a base and a dishonourable thing; yet, to resist where there is no probability, or even hopes, of our getting the better, may also be looked upon as the effect of a blind temerity, and perhaps of a weak understanding. The strokes of fortune are oftentimes as irresistible as they are severe; and he who, with an impatient reluctant spirit, fights against her, instead of alleviating, does but double her blows upon himself. A person of a quiet still tem-

per, whether it is given him by Nature, or ac-
quired by art, calmly composes himself, in the
midst of a storm, so as to elude the shock, or
receive it with the least detriment; like a prudent experienced sailor, who is swimming to
the shore from a wrecked vessel in a swelling
sea, he does not oppose the fury of the waves,
but stoops and gives way, that they may roll
over his head without obstruction. The doctrine of absolute submission in all cases is an
absurd, dogmatical precept, with nothing but
ignorance and superstition to support it: but,
upon particular occasions, and where it is impossible for us to overcome, to submit patiently is one of the most reasonable maxims
in life.

FABLE XXXIV.

THE WIND AND THE SUN.

A DISPUTE once arose betwixt the north Wind and the Sun, about the superiority of their power; and they agreed to try their strength upon a traveller, which should be able to get his cloak off first. The north Wind began, and blew a very cold blast, accompanied with a sharp driving shower. But this, and whatever else he could do, instead of making the man quit his cloak, obliged him to gird it about his body as close as possible. Next came the

Sun; who, breaking out from a thick watery cloud, drove away the cold vapours from the sky, and darted his warm sultry beams upon the head of the poor weather-beaten traveller. The man growing faint with the heat, and unable to endure it any longer, first throws off his heavy cloak, and then flies for protection to the shade of a neighbouring grove.

APPLICATION.

There is something in the temper of men so averse to severe and boisterous treatment, that he who endeavours to carry his point that way, instead of prevailing, generally leaves the mind of him, whom he has thus attempted, in a more confirmed and obstinate situation than he found it at first. Bitter words and hard usage freeze the heart into a kind of obduracy, which mild persuasion and gentle language only can dissolve and soften. Persecution has always fixed and riveted those opinions which it was intended to dispel; and some discerning men have attributed the quick growth of Christianity, in a great measure, to the rough and barbarous reception which its first teachers met with in the world. The same may have been observed of our reformation : the blood of the martyrs was the manure which produced that great protestant crop, on which the church of England has subsisted ever since. Providence, which always makes use of the most natural means to attain its purpose, has thought fit to establish the purest religion by this method: the consideration of which may give a proper check to those who are continually endeavouring to root out errors by that very management, which so infallibly fixes and implants all opinions, as well erroneous as orthodox. When an opinion is so violently attacked, it raises an attention in

the persecuted party, and gives an alarm to
their vanity, by making them think that worth
defending and keeping, at the hazard of their
lives, which, perhaps, otherwise they would
only have admired a while for the sake of its
novelty, and afterwards resigned of their own
accord. In short, a fierce turbulent opposition,
like the north Wind, only serves to make a
man wrap up his notions more closely about
him; but we know not what a kind, warm,
sun-shiny behaviour, rightly applied, would
not be able to effect.

141

FABLE XXXV.

THE KITE, THE FROG, AND THE MOUSE.

THERE was once a great emulation between the Frog and the Mouse, which should be master of the fen, and wars ensued upon it. But the crafty Mouse, lurking under the grass in ambuscade, made sudden sallies, and often surprised the enemy at a disadvantage. The Frog, excelling in strength, and being more able to leap abroad and take the field, challenged the Mouse to single combat. The Mouse accepts the challenge; and each of them entered the lists, armed with a point of a bulrush instead of a spear. A Kite, sailing in the air, beheld them afar off; and, while they were eagerly bent upon each other, and pressing on to the duel, this fatal enemy descended souse upon them, and with her crooked talons carried off both the champions.

APPLICATION.

Nothing so much exposes a man's weak side, and lays him so open to an enemy, as passion and malice. He whose attention is wholly fixed upon forming a project of revenge, is ignorant of the mischiefs that may be hatching against him from some other quarter, and upon the attack, is unprovided with the means of defending or securing himself. How are the members of a commonwealth sometimes divided amongst themselves, and inspired with rancour and malice to the last degree; and often upon as great a trifle as that which was the subject matter of debate between the Frog and the Mouse; not for any real advantage, but merely who shall get the better in the dispute? But such animosities, as insignificant and trifling as they may be among themselves, are yet of the last importance to their enemies, by giving them many fair opportunities of falling upon them, and reducing them to misery and slavery. O Britons, when will ye be wise! when will ye throw away the ridiculous distinctions of party, those ends of bulrushes, and by a prudent union secure yourselves in a state of peace and prosperity! A state, of which, if it were not for your intolerably foolish and unnecessary divisions at home, all the powers upon earth could never deprive you.

FABLE XXXVI.

THE FROGS DESIRING A KING.

T<small>HE</small> Frogs living an easy free life every where among the lakes and ponds, assembled together, one day, in a very tumultuous manner, and petitioned Jupiter to let them have a King, who might inspect their morals, and make them live a little honester. Jupiter, being at that time in pretty good humour, was pleased to laugh heartily at their ridiculous request; and, throwing a little log down into the pool, cried, ' There is a King for you.' The sudden splash which this made by its fall into the water, at first terrified them so exceedingly, that they were afraid to come near it. But in a little time, seeing it lay still without moving, they ventured, by degrees, to approach it; and at last, finding there was no danger, they leaped upon it; and, in short, treated it as familiarly as they pleased. But not contented with so insipid a King as this was, they sent their deputies to petition again for another sort of one; for this they neither did nor could like. Upon that he sent them a stork, who, without any ceremony, fell a devouring and eating them up, one after another, as fast as he could. Then they applied themselves privately to Mercury, and got him to speak to Jupiter in their behalf, that he would be so good as to bless them again with another King, or restore them to their former state. ' No,' says he, ' since it was their own choice, let the obstinate wretches suffer the punishment due to their folly.'

It is pretty extraordinary to find a fable of this kind finished with so bold and yet polite a turn by Phædrus: one who attained his freedom by the favour of Augustus, and wrote it in the time of Tiberius; who were, successively, tyrannical usurpers of the Roman government. If we may take his word for it, Æsop spoke it upon this occasion. When the commonwealth of Athens flourished under good wholesome laws of its own enacting, they relied so much upon the security of their liberty, that they negligently suffered it to run out into licentiousness. And factions happening to be fomented among them by designing people, much about the same time, Pisistratus took that opportunity to make himself master of their citadel and liberties both together. The Athenians finding themselves in a state of slavery, though their tyrant happened to be a very merciful one, yet could not bear the thoughts of it; so that Æsop, where there was no remedy, prescribes to them patience, by the example of the foregoing fable; and adds, at last, " Wherefore, my dear countrymen, be contented with your present condition, bad as it is, for fear a change should be worse."

FABLE XXXVII.

THE OLD WOMAN AND HER MAIDS.

A CERTAIN Old Woman had several Maids, whom she used to call up to their work, every morning, at the crowing of the cock. The Wenches, who found it grievous to have their sweet sleep disturbed so early, combined together, and killed the cock; thinking that, when the alarm was gone, they might enjoy themselves in their warm beds a little longer. The Old Woman, grieved for the loss of her cock, and having, by some means or other, discovered the whole plot, was resolved to be even with them; for, from that time, she obliged them to rise constantly at midnight.

APPLICATION.

It can never be expected that things should be, in all respects, agreeable to our wishes; and, if they are not very bad indeed, we ought, in many cases, to be contented with them; lest when, through impatience, we precipitately quit our present condition of life, we may to our sorrow find, with the old saying, that seldom comes a better. Before we attempt any alteration of moment, we should be certain what state it will produce; for, when things are already bad, to make them worse by trying experiments, is an argument of great weakness and folly, and is sure to be attended with a too late repentance. Grievances, if really such, ought by all means to be redressed, provided we can be assured of doing it with success: but we had better, at any time, bear with some inconvenience, than make our condition worse by attempting to mend it.

153

FABLE XXXVIII.

THE LION, THE BEAR, AND THE FOX.

A Lion and a Bear fell together by the ears over the carcase of a fawn which they found in the forest, their title to him being to be decided by force of arms. The battle was severe and tough on both sides, and they held it out, tearing and worrying one another so long, that, what with wounds and fatigue, they were so faint and weary they were not able to strike another stroke. Thus, while they lay upon the ground, panting, and lolling out their tongues,

a Fox chanced to pass by that way, who, perceiving how the case stood, very impudently
stept in between them, seized the booty which
they had all this while been contending for,
and carried it off. The two combatants, who
lay and beheld all this, without having strength
enough to stir and prevent it, were only wise
enough to make this reflection ; ' Behold the
fruits of our strife and contention! that villain,
the Fox, bears away the prize, and we ourselves
have deprived each other of the power to recover it from him.'

APPLICATION.

When people go to law about an uncertain
title, and have spent their whole estate in the
contest, nothing is more common than for some
little pettifogging attorney to step in and secure
it to himself. The very name of law seems to
imply equity and justice, and that is the bait

which has drawn in many to their ruin. Others are excited by their passions, and care not if they destroy themselves, so they do but see their enemy perish with them. But, if we lay aside prejudice and folly, and think calmly of the matter, we shall find, that going to law is not the best way of deciding differences about property ; it being, generally speaking, much safer to trust to the arbitration of two or three honest sensible neighbours, than, at a vast expence of money, time, and trouble, to run through the tedious, frivolous forms, with which, by the artifice of greedy lawyers, a court of judicature is contrived to be attended. It has been said, that if mankind would lead moral virtuous lives, there would be no occasion for divines; if they would but live temperately and soberly, that they would never want physicians: both which assertions, though true in the main, are yet expressed in too great a latitude. But one may venture to affirm, that if men preserved a strict regard to justice and honesty in their dealings with each other, and upon any mistake or misapprehension were always ready to refer the matter to disinterested umpires, of acknowledged judgment and integrity, they never could have the least occasion for lawyers. When people have gone to law, it is rarely to be found but one or both parties was either stupidly obstinate, or rashly inconsiderate, For, if the case should happen to be so intricate that a man of common sense could not distinguish who had the best title, how easy would it be to have the opinion of the best counsel in the land, and agree to determine it by that? If it should appear dubious even after that, how much better would it be to divide the thing in dispute, rather than go to law, and hazard the losing not only of the whole, but costs and damages into the bargain?

157

FABLE XXXIX.

THE CROW AND THE PITCHER.

A Crow, ready to die with thirst, flew with joy to a Pitcher, which he beheld at some distance. When he came, he found water in it indeed, but so near the bottom, that, with all his stooping and straining, he was not able to reach it. Then he endeavoured to overturn the Pitcher, that so at least he might be able to get a little of it. But his strength was not sufficient for this. At last, seeing some pebbles lie near the place, he cast them one

by one into the Pitcher; and thus, by degrees,
raised the water up to the very brim, and satisfied his thirst.

APPLICATION.

Many things which cannot be effected by
strength, or by the vulgar way of enterprising,
may yet be brought about by some new and
untried means. A man of sagacity and penetration, upon encountering a difficulty or two,
does not immediately despair; but, if he cannot succeed one way, employs his wit and
ingenuity another; and, to avoid or get over
an impediment, makes no scruple of stepping
out of the path of his forefathers. Since our
happiness, next to the regulation of our minds,
depends altogether upon our having and enjoying the conveniences of life, why should
we stand upon ceremony about the methods
of obtaining them, or pay any deference to

antiquity upon that score? If almost every age had not exerted itself in some new improvements of its own, we should want a thousand arts, or, at least, many degrees of perfection in every art, which at present we are in possession of. The invention of any thing which is more commodious for the mind or body than what they had before, ought to be embraced readily, and the projector of it distinguished with a suitable encouragement. Such as the use of the compass, for example, from which mankind reaps so much benefit and advantage, and which was not known to former ages. When we follow the steps of those who have gone before us in the old beaten track of life, how do we differ from horses in a team, which are linked to each other by a chain or harness, and move on in a dull heavy pace, to the tune of their leader's bells? But the man who enriches the present fund of knowledge with some new and useful improvement, like a happy adventurer at sea, discovers, as it were, an unknown land, and imports an additional trade into his own country.

FABLE XL.

THE PORCUPINE AND THE SNAKES.

A PORCUPINE, wanting to shelter himself, desired a nest of Snakes to give him admittance
into their cave. They were prevailed upon, and
let him in accordingly; but were so annoyed
with his sharp prickly quills that they soon re-
pented of their easy compliance, and entreated
the Porcupine to withdraw, and leave them
their hole to themselves. 'No,' says he, 'let
them quit the place that don't like it; for my
part, I am well enough satisfied as I am.'

APPLICATION

Some people are of so brutish, inhospitable tempers, that there is no living with them, without greatly incommoding ourselves. Therefore, before we enter into any degree of friendship, alliance, or partnership, with any person whatever, we should thoroughly consider his nature and qualities, his circumstances and his humour. There ought to be something in each of these respects to tally and correspond with our own measures, to suit our genius, and adapt itself to the size and proportion of our desires, otherwise our associations, of whatever kind, may prove the greatest plagues of our life. Young men are very apt to run into this error; and being warm in all their passions, throw open their arms at once, and admit into the greatest intimacy persons whom they know little of, but by false and uncertain lights. Thus they sometimes receive a Viper into their bosom instead of a friend, and take a Porcupine for a consort, with whom they are obliged to cohabit, though she may prove a thorn in their sides as long as they live. A true friend is one of the greatest blessings in life; therefore to be mistaken or disappointed of such enjoyment, when we hope to be in full possession of it, must be as great a mortification. So that we cannot be too nice and scrupulous in our choice of those who are to be our companions for life: for they must have but a poor shallow notion of friendship who intend to take it, like a lease, for a term of years only. In a word, the doctrine which this fable speaks, is to prepare us against being injured or deceived by a rash combination of any sort. The manners of the man we desire for a friend, of the woman we like for a wife, of the person with whom we would jointly manage and concert measures for the advancement of our temporal interest, should be narrowly and cautiously inspected, before we embark with them in the same vessel, lest we should alter our mind when it is too late, and think of regaining the shore after we have launched out of our depth.

FABLE XLI.

THE HARES AND FROGS IN A STORM.

Upon a great storm of wind that blew among the trees and bushes, and made a rustling with the leaves, the Hares (in a certain park where there happened to be a plenty of them) were so terribly frighted that they run like mad all over the place, resolving to seek out some retreat of more security, or to end their unhappy days by doing violence to themselves. With this resolution they found an outlet where a pale had been broken down, and, bolting forth upon an adjoining common, had not run far before their course was stopt by that of a gentle brook which glided across the way they intended to take. This was so grievous a disappointment that they were not able to bear it; and they determined rather to throw themselves headlong into the water, let what would become of it, than lead a life so full of dangers and crosses. But, upon their coming to the brink of the river, a parcel of Frogs, which were sitting there, frighted at their approach, leapt into the stream in great confusion, and dived to the very bottom for fear: which a cunning old puss observing, called to the rest and said, ' Hold, have a care what ye do: here are other creatures, I perceive, which have their fears as well as us: don't then let us fancy ourselves the most miserable of any upon earth; but rather, by their example, learn to bear patiently those inconveniences which our nature has thrown upon us,'

167

APPLICATION.

This fable is designed to shew us how unreasonable many people are for living in such
continual fears and disquiets about the miser-
ableness of their condition. There is hardly
any state of life great enough to satisfy the
wishes of an ambitious man; and scarce any so
mean but may supply all the necessities of him
that is moderate. But if people will be so un-
wise as to work themselves up to imaginary
misfortunes, why do they grumble at nature
and their stars, when their own perverse minds
are only to blame? If we are to conclude ourselves unhappy by as many degrees as there
are others greater than we, why then the greatest part of mankind must be miserable, in some
degree at least. But, if they who repine at
their own afflicted condition would but reckon
up how many more there are with whom they
would not change cases, than whose pleasures

they envy, they would certainly rise up better satisfied from such a calculation. But what shall we say to those who have a way of creating themselves panics from the rustling of the wind, the scratching of a rat or mouse behind the hangings, the fluttering of a moth, or the motion of their own shadow by moonlight? Their whole life is as full of alarms as that of a Hare, and they never think themselves so happy as when, like the timorous folks in the fable, they meet with a set of creatures as fearful as themselves.

169

FABLE XLII.

THE FOX AND THE WOLF.

THE Wolf having laid in store of provision, kept close at home, and made much of himself. The Fox observed this, and thinking it something particular, went to visit him, the better to inform himself of the truth of the matter. The Wolf excused himself from seeing him, by pretending he was very much indisposed. All this did but confirm the Fox in his suspicions: so away he goes to a shepherd, and made discovery of the Wolf; telling him, he

.

had nothing else to do but to come with a good weapon and knock him on the head as he lay in his cave. The shepherd followed his directions, and killed the Wolf. The wicked Fox enjoyed the cave and provisions to himself, but enjoyed them not long; for the same shepherd passing afterwards by the same hole, and seeing the Fox there, dispatched him also.

APPLICATION.

This fable seems to be directed against the odious trade of informing. Not that giving in informations against criminals and enemies of the public is in itself odious, for it is commendable; but the circumstances and manner of doing it oftentimes make it a vile and detestable employment. He that accuses another merely for the sake of the promised reward, or in hopes of getting his forfeited estate, or with any other such mercenary view, nay, even to

save his own life, whatever he gets by the bargain, is sure to lose his reputation; for, indeed,
the most innocent company is not safe with
such a one in it, nor the neighbourhood secure
in which he lives. A villain of his stamp,
whose only end is getting, will as soon betray
the innocent as the guilty: let him but know
where there is a suspected person, and propose
the reward, and he will scarce fail to work the
suspicion up to high treason, or be at a loss to
give sufficient proofs of it. We have no small
comfort concerning this sort of people, when
we consider how improbable it is that they
should thrive or prosper long in their ill-gotten
possessions. For he that can betray another
for the sake of a little pelf, must be a man of
such bad principles that it cannot be for the
interest of any community to suffer him to live
long in it. Besides, he himself will not be contented with one single villany; and there is no

fear but he will provoke justice to hurl down upon his head at least as great a calamity as he, by his malicious information, has brought upon another.

173

FABLE XLIII.

THE DOG AND THE SHEEP.

The Dog sued the Sheep for a debt, of which the kite and the wolf were to be judges. They, without debating long upon the matter, or making any scruple for want of evidence, gave sentence for the plaintiff; who immediately tore the poor Sheep in pieces, and divided the spoil with the unjust judges.

APPLICATION.

Deplorable are the times when open bare-faced villany is protected and encouraged, when innocence is obnoxious, honesty contemptible, and it is reckoned criminal to espouse the cause of virtue. Men originally entered into covenants and civil compacts with each other for the promotion of their happiness and well-being, for the establishment of justice and public peace. How comes it then that they look stupidly on, and tamely acquiesce, when wicked men pervert this end, and establish an arbitrary tyranny of their own, upon the foundation of fraud and oppression? Among beasts, who are incapable of being civilized by social laws, it is no strange thing to see innocent helpless sheep fall a prey to dogs, wolves, and kites: but it is amazing how mankind could ever sink down to such a low degree of base cowardice, as to suffer some of the worst of their species to usurp a power over them, to supersede the righteous laws of good government, and to exercise all kinds of injustice and hardship, in gratifying their own vicious lusts. Wherever such enormities are practised, it is when a few rapacious statesmen combine together to get and secure the power in their own hands, and agree to divide the spoils among themselves. For as long as the cause is to be tried only among themselves, no question but they will always vouch for each other. But, at the same time, it is hard to determine which resemble brutes most, they in acting, or the people in suffering them to act, their vile selfish schemes.

FABLE XLIV.

THE PEACOCK AND THE CRANE.

The Peacock and the Crane by chance met together in the same place. The Peacock erecting his tail, displayed his gaudy plumes, and looked with contempt upon the Crane, as some mean ordinary person. The Crane, resolving to mortify his insolence, took occasion to say, that Peacocks were very fine birds indeed, if fine feathers could make them so; but that he thought it a much nobler thing to be able to rise above the clouds, than to strut about upon the ground, and be gazed at by children.

APPLICATION.

It is very absurd to slight or insult another upon his wanting a property which we possess; for he may, for any thing we know, have as just reason to triumph over us, by being master of some good quality of which we are incapable. But, in regard to the fable before us, that which the Peacock values himself upon, the glitter and finery of dress, is one of the most trifling considerations in nature; and what a man of sense would be ashamed to reckon even as the least part of merit. Indeed, children, and those people who think much about the same pitch with them, are apt to be taken with varnish and tinsel; but they, who examine by the scale of common sense must find something of weight and substance, before they can be persuaded to set a value. The mind which is stored with virtuous and rational sentiments, and the behaviour which speaks complacence and humility, stamps an estimate upon the professor, which all judicious spectators are ready to admire and acknowledge. But if there be any merit in an embroidered coat, a brocade waistcoat, a shoe, a stocking, or a sword-knot, the person who wears them has the least claim to it; let it be ascribed where if justly belongs—to the several artisans who wrought and disposed the materials of which they consist. This moral is not intended to derogate any thing from the magnificence of fine clothes and rich equipages, which, as times and circumstances require, may be used with decency and propriety enough : but one cannot help being concerned, lest any worth should be affixed to them more than their own intrinsic value.

181

FABLE XLV.

THE VIPER AND THE FILE.

A Viper entering a smith's shop, looked up
and down for something to eat; and seeing a
File, fell to gnawing it as greedily as could be.
The File told him, very gruffly, that he had
best be quiet and let him alone; for he would
get very little by nibbling at one who, upon
occasion, could bite iron and steel.

APPLICATION.

By this fable we are cautioned to consider
what any person is, before we make an attack

upon him after any manner whatsoever: particularly how we let our tongues slip in censuring the actions of those who are, in the opinion of the world, not only of an unquestioned reputation, so that nobody will believe what we insinuate against them; but of such an influence, upon account of their own veracity, that the least word from them would ruin our credit to all intents and purposes. If wit be the case, and we have a satirical vein, which at certain periods must have a flow, let us be cautious at whom we level it; for if the person's understanding be of better proof than our own, all our ingenious sallies, like liquor squirted against the wind, will recoil back upon our own faces, and make us the ridicule of every spectator. This fable, besides, is not an improper emblem of envy; which, rather than not bite at all, will fall foul where it can hurt nothing but itself.

183

FABLE XLVI.

THE ASS, THE LION, AND THE COCK.

An Ass and a Cock happened to be feeding together in the same place, when on a sudden they spied a Lion approaching them. This beast is reported, above all things, to have an aversion, or rather antipathy, to the crowing of a Cock; so that he no sooner heard the voice of that bird, but he betook him to his heels, and ran away as fast as ever he could. The Ass fancying he fled for fear of him, in the bravery of his heart pursued him, and followed him so far, that they were quite out of the hearing of the Cock; which the Lion no sooner perceived, but he turned about and seized the Ass; and just as he was ready to tear him to pieces, the sluggish creature is said to have expressed himself thus:—' Alas! fool that I was, knowing the cowardice of my own nature, thus by an affected courage to throw myself into the jaws of death, when I might have remained secure and unmolested!'

APPLICATION.

There are many who, out of an ambition to appear considerable, affect to shew themselves men of fire, spirit, and courage: but these being qualities, of which they are not the right owners, they generally expose themselves, and shew the little title they have to them, by endeavouring to exert and produce them at unseasonable times, or with improper persons. A bully, for fear you should find him out to be a coward, overacts his part, and calls you to account for affronts which a man of true bravery would never have thought of: and a cowardly silly fellow, observing that he may take some liberties with impunity, where perhaps the place or the company protect him, falsely concludes from thence, that the person with whom he made free is a greater coward than himself; so that he not only continues his offensive raillery and impertinence for the present, but probably renews them in some place not so privileged as the former, where his insolence meets with a due chastisement; than which nothing is more equitable in itself, or agreeable to the discreet part of mankind.

187

FABLE XLVII.

THE JACKDAW AND PEACOCKS.

A CERTAIN Jackdaw was so proud and ambitious, that, not contented to live within his
own sphere, he picked up the feathers which
fell from the Peacocks, stuck them in among
his own, and very confidently introduced himself into an assembly of those beautiful birds.
They soon found him out, stripped him of his
borrowed plumes, and, falling upon him with
their sharp bills, punished him as his presump-
tion deserved. Upon this, full of grief and

affliction, he returned to his old companions, and would have flocked with them again; but they, knowing his late life and conversation, industriously avoided him, and refused to admit him into their company; and one of them, at the same time, gave him this serious reproof—' If, friend, you could have been contented with our station, and had not disdained the rank in which Nature had placed you, you had not been used so scurvily by those upon whom you intruded yourself, nor suffered the notorious slight which now we think ourselves obliged to put upon you.'

APPLICATION.

What we may learn from this fable is, in the main, to live contentedly in our own condition, whatever it be, without affecting to look bigger than we are by a false or borrowed light. To be barely pleased with appearing above what a man really is, is bad enough; and what may justly render him contemptible in the eyes of his equals: but if, to enable him to do this with something of a better grace, he has clandestinely feathered his nest with his neighbour's goods, when found out, he has nothing to expect but to be stripped of his plunder, and used like a felonious rogue into the bargain.

END OF THE FIRST VOLUME.

T. Bensiey, Printer,
Bolt Court, Fleet Street, London.